MW00466972

Murder in a Library

By Charles J. Dutton

Originally published in 1931

Murder in a Library

© 2013 Resurrected Press
www.ResurrectedPress.com

All rights reserved. No part of this book may be used or reproduced in any manner without written permission except for brief quotations for review purposes.

Published by Intrepid Ink, LLC

Intrepid Ink, LLC provides full publishing services to authors of fiction and non-fiction books, eBooks and websites. From editing to formatting, to publishing, to marketing, Intrepid Ink gets your creative works into the hands of the people who want to read them.
Find out more at www.IntrepidInk.com.

ISBN 13: 978-1-937022-62-4

Printed in the United States of America

RESURRECTED PRESS CLASSIC MYSTERY CATALOGUE

Journeys into Mystery
Travel and Mystery in a More Elegant Time

The Edwardian Detectives
Literary Sleuths of the Edwardian Era

Gems of Mystery
Lost Jewels from a More Elegant Age

Anne Austin
One Drop of Blood
The Black Pigeon
Murder at Bridge

E. C. Bentley
Trent's Last Case: The Woman in Black

Ernest Bramah
Max Carrados Resurrected:
The Detective Stories of Max Carrados

Agatha Christie
The Secret Adversary
The Mysterious Affair at Styles

Octavus Roy Cohen
Midnight

Freeman Wills Croft
The Ponson Case
The Pit Prop Syndicate

J. S. Fletcher
The Herapath Property
The Rayner-Slade Amalgamation
The Chestermarke Instinct
The Paradise Mystery
Dead Men's Money
The Middle of Things
Ravensdene Court
Scarhaven Keep
The Orange-Yellow Diamond
The Middle Temple Murder
The Tallyrand Maxim
The Borough Treasurer
In the Mayor's Parlour
The Saftey Pin

R. Austin Freeman
The Mystery of 31 New Inn from the Dr. Thorndyke Series
John Thorndyke's Cases from the Dr. Thorndyke Series
The Red Thumb Mark from The Dr. Thorndyke Series
The Eye of Osiris from The Dr. Thorndyke Series
A Silent Witness from the Dr. John Thorndyke Series
The Cat's Eye from the Dr. John Thorndyke Series
Helen Vardon's Confession: A Dr. John Thorndyke Story
As a Thief in the Night: A Dr. John Thorndyke Story
Mr. Pottermack's Oversight: A Dr. John Thorndyke Story
Dr. Thorndyke Intervenes: A Dr. John Thorndyke Story
The Singing Bone: The Adventures of Dr. Thorndyke
The Stoneware Monkey: A Dr. John Thorndyke Story
The Great Portrait Mystery, and Other Stories: A Collection of Dr. John Thorndyke and Other Stories
The Penrose Mystery: A Dr. John Thorndyke Story
The Uttermost Farthing: A Savant's Vendetta

Dorothy L. Sayers
Whose Body?

Sir William Magnay
The Hunt Ball Mystery

Mabel and Paul Thorne
The Sheridan Road Mystery

Louis Tracy
The Strange Case of Mortimer Fenley
The Albert Gate Mystery
The Bartlett Mystery
The Postmaster's Daughter
The House of Peril
The Sandling Case: What Would You Have Done?

Charles Edmonds Walk
The Paternoster Ruby

John R. Watson
The Mystery of the Downs
The Hampstead Mystery

Edgar Wallace
The Daffodil Mystery
The Crimson Circle

Carolyn Wells
Vicky Van
The Man Who Fell Through the Earth
In the Onyx Lobby
Raspberry Jam
The Clue
The Room with the Tassels
The Vanishing of Betty Varian
The Mystery Girl
The White Alley

The Curved Blades
Anybody but Anne
The Bride of a Moment
Faulkner's Folly
The Diamond Pin
The Gold Bag
The Mystery of the Sycamore
The Come Back

Raoul Whitfield
Death in a Bowl

And much more!
Visit ResurrectedPress.com
for our complete catalogue

FOREWORD

The 1920's and 1930's are one of the most interesting periods in the history of detective fiction. On the one hand, it was the "Golden Age" of British mysteries with such authors as Agatha Christie, Dorothy L. Sayers, Anthony Berkeley along with many others producing a body of work that was both literate and genteel. The emphasis was on the puzzle element of the crime, with authors vying with each other to create the most ingenious methods of murder. On the other side of the Atlantic, authors such as Carroll John Daly, Dashiell Hammett, and Raymond Chandler were inventing a far different type of detective fiction. This hard-boiled school focused on the seamier aspects of society where the success of the detective depended more on his abilities with fist and gun than cleverness.

Yet not all authors of mysteries can be so easily classified as belonging to one camp or the other. This was particularly true in America where many authors adopted aspects of both styles in their works. Charles J. Dutton was one of these authors.

On the surface, Dutton would seem an unlikely author of mysteries. University educated, he studied both the law and theology. He worked for a period of time as a journalist before finally taking up a post as minister in a church in Iowa. While a minister, he was a frequent contributor to of uplifting articles to *The Reader's Digest*. Yet, in the 20's and early 30's he authored sixteen mystery novels as well as numerous short stories. His works have none of the raw violence that characterize the hard-boiled school, but, written for the most part during the era of Prohibition, there is a dark undercurrent of crime and lawlessness below the "respectable" society on which the books are centered.

His early works feature John Bartley, who as a detective, is in some ways almost a throwback to the Edwardian examples of the profession. A man of means, education, and breeding, he solves the crimes of the wealthy and powerful by force of intellect. But even Bartley finds himself involved with subjects that were taboo for many authors of the era, such as racism and religious fundamentalism. This is particularly true in the novel *The Crooked Cross*.

His second series of mysteries, of which this volume is one, focus on Harley Manners, a professor of abnormal and criminal psychology. Rather than the "How", Professor Manners is much more concerned with the "Why" a crime was committed. His success as an investigator owes as much to his understanding of the human mind, particularly its dark side, as to physical clues. The villains in the six books of the series are motivated as much by a psychological pathology as by greed or lust. As if to accentuate this dual nature of good and evil, his two best friends are Rogan the chief of police and Zuko, a prominent underworld figure.

Murder in a Library deals with a crime in a place normally considered a haven of peace and especially quiet, a public library. A librarian, a sixty year old spinster, is murdered in her office while dozens of people peruse books and magazines in the reading room just outside the door. With no clues and no obvious motive, the crime baffles the local police. Only when Professor manners becomes involved is a solution found.

While somewhat forgotten as a mystery writer today, Charles J. Dutton was an author who could look into the darker side of human nature. For this reason his novels should still be of interest to the modern reader. It is therefore, with pleasure that Resurrected Press introduces this new edition of *Murder in a Library*.

About the Author

Charles J. Dutton (1888-1964) was an American writer of mysteries. He was educated at Brown University and later studied at Albany Law School and the Defiance Theological Seminary. After graduation he worked for a while as a newspaper columnist. He wrote numerous works of fiction that were published in magazines both in the U.S. and Great Britain. In the early 1930's he moved to Des Moines, Iowa where he assumed the post of minister for the First Unitarian Church. He wrote some fifteen mystery novels. Appearing in nine of these was the private detective John Bartley. Bartley was followed by Professor Harley Manners, a criminal psychologist who was featured in six novels. The two characters overlap in the book *Streaked With Crimson*. One of the things that set Dutton apart from other mystery writers of the period was his interest in the psychology of the criminal mind. He was also fascinated by old books and ancient history, subjects which play parts in a number of his novels.

Greg Fowlkes
Editor-In-Chief
Resurrected Press
www.ResurrectedPress.com

CHAPTER ONE

With his back pressed close against the door of the police station, Carty Rand stood gloomily staring across the street. Should he go up to the Press Club and play poker with the gang, or spend the next hour improving his mind in the public library? The Press Club meant walking three long blocks in the rain; as for the library, all he had to do was to walk across the street.

A few weeks before, the city editor had called Rand into the office to break the news that for the next few months the young reporter was to do police work, and had suggested that he might also cover the library. No two assignments could have pleased Rand better. Police work had always thrilled him and, like every other newspaper man, some day he was going to write a novel.

With his soft hat pulled low over his eyes, the usual cigarette in the corner of his lips, he stood looking out at the wet afternoon. It had been raining hard all day and evidently would do the same all night. The street was a glittering surface of moisture, and, whipped by a steady wind, the rain lashed in blinding sheets around the police station.

Making up his mind that the Press Club was too far away, he blessed the city fathers who had placed the public buildings in a civic center on the river front. For half a mile on both sides of the dirty river ran a strip of green grass; behind it stood the municipal buildings; across the water he could see the two granite court houses.

On a bright day, the green grass, the river and the stone buildings which flanked the promenade made a rather pleasing picture, but as he looked out at the blinding rain, Carty Rand decided it was not only an ugly scene but also a very depressing one. The buildings were streaked with moisture and every hideous corner and^angle leaped forth to meet his eyes. With a despairing shrug of his shoulders the tall young man pulled his coat collar up around his neck and darted down the steps of the police station. As he ran across the street the rain slapped against his face, and once he slipped and almost fell. Up the five stone steps of the library entrance he hurried, pausing for breath before the main door.

Though it was one of the best known public libraries in the country, famous for its efficient management and public service, yet the building itself was old and much out of date. Once, some forgotten architect had thought the squatty granite structure a thing of beauty, but that was in a day long past. To Rand it was the most hideous building in the city.

Inside the door he climbed the three steps and came into the main lobby of the library. It was a large square room containing several couches, with easychairs flanking book-laden tables. To his right was the delivery desk, behind it the long rows of stacks, and on his left the desk where the books were checked out. Above his head ran a book-lined balcony. On the walls were several large, though not very beautiful, paintings.

Crossing the floor he paused at the delivery desk and for a few moments joked with the efficient looking girl who was in charge. Because of the storm the room was almost deserted and the assistant had plenty of time at her disposal. There were at least twenty girls on the staff and Rand knew them all, for there was hardly a day during which he did not drop into the building.

The conversation over, he paused by the open door of the librarian's office and threw a quick look into the room. Behind a rosewood desk he saw the short figure of the man who controlled the reading tastes of the city. As a rule Rand dropped into the office for a few moments' chat, but the librarian was engaged in a conversation, so Rand drifted past the door toward the reading room. This was the largest room in the building and, as he passed through the open doors, he saw that it was filled. On every side were tall bookcases whose volumes made a pleasing contrast of colors. The tables were all occupied, and most of the magazines had been taken down from the racks. Over the room hung that uneasy stillness which one finds in a room filled with silent people.

Though books were Rand's chief hobby, yet he did not feel like reading. After all, it was the rain which had brought him into the library—the rain and the fact that the Press Club was seven long blocks away. There were at least two hours to be killed, and picking out a book of modern verse from the nearest case, he sank down into a chair.

For a while he tried to read, then, in sheer boredom, allowed the book to drop down upon the table. Reading, he decided, was the last thing he wanted to do, so he began to study the people in the room, people who, in many cases, were making no more attempt at reading than he was.

The reading room of a public library brings together many varying types of people. There are always those who have come for reference purposes, groups of high school boys and girls with a scattering of college students. These, Rand discovered when he looked over the room, were absent. But another class was well represented.

Because it is in a public building, warm and well lighted, and containing plenty of free reading matter, the reference room of every library brings together a large number of homeless men and women. The casual tramps, outcasts and petty criminals, the old and defeated in life spend many hours in the public reading room.

Rand was an intelligent young newspaper man, but it would have required little intelligence to place the groups sitting at the tables—men in faded, soiled and dingy suits, some with sly shifty faces, others who kept darting quick glances at the many tables. The outcasts and the homeless had been driven by the storm into the warm room.

For a time he studied the people around him. Some of the occupants of the tables he had seen in the police courts. He half smiled as he noticed one of the city's leading clergymen sitting beside a thin, shrunken figure who had come out of prison only three days before. There were several there who had been in jail, and a few who he knew would be there some day.

He gazed for a while languidly around. It was four o'clock and on a clear day the high school students would by now be thronging in through the big doors, but the rain had kept them away. The girl behind the reference desk was having nothing to do and, seated at her desk, she was carefully reading a magazine.

It was a silent room except when someone turned the pages of a paper or scraped his feet across the floor. Once in a while there was a cough, checked as a rule almost the moment it sounded forth. From outside came the sound of the rain dashing over the windows, the howling of the wind as it shrieked its way around the building.

It was after he had listened to the rain for some time that Rand began to feel uneasy. There was not the slightest reason why he should be disturbed, but he was. The silence seemed suspicious. He caught himself waiting for someone to whisper to his neighbor. To throw aside this feeling, he began to watch a man seated at the other side of the room. It was an oddly shaped room. Three fourths of it was a large square, the floor filled with tables, the walls lined with bookcases. The other fourth was filled with high magazine racks. Behind them was a half hidden office, its sides enclosed with frosted glass and with a little narrow door.

This built-in room was the office of the woman who had charge of the reading room. Rand knew her well and, unlike most of the people of the city, was a favorite of the thin, angular and rather ill-tempered old lady. For thirty-five years the reference room had been her kingdom, and the years of detailed work had not improved her disposition. Yet for some reason, perhaps because she had known his mother, Ruby Merton had taken a liking to the unconventional reporter. She had two assistants, and was not often seen outside of her enclosed office, but everyone in the city knew the old lady, and her sharp tongue had made her a public character. Few were the persons ever invited to pass behind the frosted glass partitions and sit beside her large desk.

For the past ten minutes Rand had noticed that Joe White was much interested in the door of the librarian's office. Every reporter knew Joe—just as the police knew him well. He was a petty sneak thief who found it a hard task to keep on the water wagon. Not only was he a thief but also a bit of a coward, sneaking and sniveling his way through life and always in trouble.

Seated at a table, the thin little figure was holding a newspaper before his face. But at the angle in which he was sitting, Rand was able to see the sharp, sallow features. Again and again he saw the man throw a quick eager questioning look at the office door, a look which would be repeated in a few moments. For some reason Joe was interested in the glass-enclosed office.

Having nothing else to do, Rand picked up a magazine and made a bluff at reading. It was only a gesture, for he was watching the police character. Why White was in the library he knew. The wind and the storrm had driven him to warmth and shelter. But why he should appear so interested in the glass-enclosed room he could not understand. That he was interested there was no doubt. Again and again the narrow shifting eyes would dart a quick look at the door. It was a curious look, filled with both wonder and anticipation, as though he was watching for someone to come into the larger room. After each glance at the door, Rand noticed that White would throw a searching look around the tables, as if trying to see if he had been observed. That White was up to any serious mischief the reporter doubted. There were at least fifty people in the reading room, and one could not move without being observed, but something had aroused the curiosity of the sneak thief, and he seemed to be a little bit excited.

At last Rand rose slowly to his feet. Walking across the floor, he paused for a moment before the magazine rack and threw a long look at White. The little figure had given Rand a suspicious glance, but when Rand looked at him the thin face was quickly buried in the paper. With a slight smile the reporter passed behind the long magazine rack and a second later stood before the door of the office.

The door was closed and he paused for a moment wondering if should open it. He was standing in an open space behind the tall magazine racks. In front of him were the frosted glass partitions, to his right the wall with the two large windows. On every side were bookcases.

As his hand shot out for the knob, he hesitated for a moment. Again there swept over him the queer uneasy feeling he had experienced a few moments ago. It was an odd feeling, one he was unable to analyze. It made him wonder what could be the matter with his nerves. Above his head the rain was smearing across the windows. He cast a sudden glance toward the little table, and his look caused the watching eyes of White to drop quickly to the paper he held in his hand.

With a shrug of his shoulders Rand opened the door and looked into the glass-enclosed room. Across from him was another door which he thought led out into a hallway. On two sides of the room were tall bookcases filled with bulky reference works and piles of magazines. Three steps would have brought him to the desk, littered with papers and book catalogues, but the eyes of the young man narrowed as he saw the woman slumped down in the chair behind the desk.

No one had ever called the reference librarian good-looking; there were many who said she was just the opposite. Eccentric in everything she did, like many of her type, her clothes ran to vivid, extreme colors. The purple dress did give the room a touch of color, but Rand did not notice the dress. There was something which puzzled him.

The woman was seated behind her desk, but the angular figure had slumped down far into her chair. She was sitting in an odd and uncomfortable position and something about her appearance caused him to catch his breath suddenly. He could not see her face, for her head had fallen forward, and only the closecropped hair could be observed. He noticed that she was very still.

For a moment he stood silent in the doorway. Then all at once the sound of rain upon the windows seemed to die away. Nor did he hear the rustling of papers in the reading room. A curious silence seemed to brood over the little room—a silence which he could feel pressing around him in a sinister manner. Then suddenly giving a gasp he stepped quickly into the room, carefully shutting the door behind him.

By the chair he stood looking down at the still, pathetic figure. Though he had made some slight noise in crossing the floor, she had not raised her head. As he looked down at the purple dress, and saw the thin white hair upon her head, he suddenly realized that she would never raise her eyes to look at him. It was at this second that he saw the cord around her neck.

It was not a pleasant sight. Drawn tightly around the swollen throat, it was pulled so taut that it was hard to distinguish it. His eyes fell upon a knife lying upon the desk, but as he picked it up and reached down to cut the cord he knew that the effort was useless. The woman was dead and had been dead for some time.

He managed at length to cut the encircling cord and silently placed it upon the desk. Accustomed as he was to scenes of violence, yet he shuddered as he carefully raised the woman's head with his hand. One look at the wild, staring eyes, the pain-twisted face, and he trembled.

His first instinctive impulse was to rush from the room and shout for aid, but he did not move. He was a reporter and had stumbled upon what might prove to be the most sensational crime story of the year. And it was his own personal story—a real beat.

He had known the librarian for some years. To others she might have been sarcastic, even rude; to him she had been kindly and helpful. That any person in the city would take her life seemed beyond belief, yet before him, slumped in that odd attitude in the chair, was her silent figure.

That it was murder there was no doubt. The cord had been drawn so tightly around her neck that it had cut the flesh. What was more, the slip knot was at the back. A finger shot out for a moment to touch the swollen face. It was still warm. Death had come within the past hour. As he thought this, he gave a start.

Out in the reading room were at least fifty people. All afternoon the room had been filled, the tables and chairs occupied. It was a motley group that had been driven to shelter by the rain, the outcasts and failures and the petty criminals of the city streets. Yet it seemed incredible that she could have been killed with help only a few feet away, murdered only a few minutes before without any of the fifty persons in the next room aware of what was being done.

He cast a slow somber look beyond the desk. Against the wall stood a large green safe, its doors partly open. In the dark interior he saw a row of shelves, the backs of books. But the safe held his gaze for only a second. The telephone upon the desk was within reach of his hand. Sinking down in a chair he took the receiver from the hook and called a number.

As he waited for his connection, he felt grateful for one thing. Across the street was the police station, and the head of the homicide squad was in his office. Rand was glad of that, for Kent was a shrewd, efficient police official. As he was thinking this, the connection was made; a second later he heard the rough voice of the inspector.

"Listen, chief," came Rand's low voice, "it's Rand, over in the library. Yes, the library. Now listen carefully. Someone has just done in Ruby Merton. Yes, that's what I said. It's a killing. I stumbled on her body. No one knows a thing about it yet, I just found her. Rush over here and bring some dicks with you. There's a big bunch in the reading room. You will want to line them up. Yes—"

He paused a moment to listen to the sharp barking questions, picturing the surprised official at the other end of the wire. Just as Kent was about to slam down the receiver Rand spoke again. "Now listen to this, chief. If you see Joe White sliding out of the building, pick him up. I'll give you the low down later. Yes, it's the office in the reading room. And hurry over. It's a bit lonesome in here just now."

Rand held the receiver in his hand for several moments after he heard the inspector slam down his instrument. Soberly his eyes went traveling around the little room. As they passed over the silent figure in the chair he shook his head. People talked about the dignity of death. There was none here. An old lady who had given her life to the service of the public had died, died by violence, with more than fifty people within sound of her voice.

CHAPTER TWO

The telephone receiver remained upon the hook only a second. As Rand's glance fell upon the wall clock he remembered that he was a reporter, and that the last evening edition would be going to print in a few moments. Calling the city room, he asked for the managing editor, knowing that for the first time in his career he was giving his chief a real beat. The connection completed, there followed a short, snappy conversation. There was much to tell; he had stumbled upon a crime; that crime was murder. Before the busy editor got off the line he told Rand to stick to the story until the case was solved.

Replacing the receiver, Rand rose to his feet, studying the room. So far as he could see there was nothing out of the way. The doors of the big green safe were wide open, and he tried to remember if they had been open on the other occasions when he had been in the office.

Out in the reading room there was a sound of hurrying footsteps; the door was flung open and the tall, raw-boned figure of the police inspector stood on the threshold. Behind him was the police doctor.The gray eyes of the official rested for a second upon the face of the reporter, then passed over to the silent figure at the desk, and Rand saw the square jaw shut tight as the dead woman came into the inspector's vision. After a moment's silence he stepped into the room, followed by the doctor. As the inspector raised the woman's head he asked Rand to close the door. With his back against the door Rand watched the two police officials make a quick but careful examination of the body. No one spoke, and within the little room was silence; but from behind the door came the murmur of excited voices, loud whisperings and shuffling feet. The reporter could picture the amazed room watching the police walk across the floor. Perhaps someone in that room had reason to fear them. Straightening up, Kent made a quick inspection of the little office with his keen gray eyes. The glance ended at the surface of the desk, and the cord which Rand had thrown upon a magazine met his eyes.

Picking it up, the inspector gave it one glance. For a moment there was silence; then Kent turned to the reporter.

"Tell me how you happened to find her," he commanded.

There was not much to tell and the story was soon ended. Kent made no effort to break in, and while Rand was talking the inspector's eyes were carefully studying the office. Not until Rand paused was there a question.

"You say Joe White made you suspicious?"

"Got me guessing why he was so interested in the office. That's why I got up and came in. I knew the old lady pretty well."

Kent started to speak, then turned and looked at his doctor. Rand knew the young physician and was glad the police had someone of intelligence for their medical man, instead of the usual inefficient political appointee. As the doctor carefully allowed the woman's head to fall back upon her breast, the inspector spoke:

"What about it, Trent?"

"Strangled. The murderer placed the cord around her neck and just pulled it tight. Been dead more than thirty minutes."

Rand saw the brows of the inspector knit as the man looked in the direction of the reading room.

A puzzled look swept over his face as he slowly shook his head.

"There were fifty or sixty people in that room when we walked through. She must have been killed here, yet I have a hunch we will find no one heard a sound. That's what I can't see."

"But Kent," came the doctor's low tones. "It's my idea she had a hand pressed down over her lips, so that she wasn't able to scream. You see she could not have been very strong."

Whatever Kent thought of this statement his next remark had nothing to do with what had just been said. He asked the doctor to find the librarian, to tell him what had taken place, and arrange to have the library closed. No one was to be allowed to enter the building nor was anyone to leave the place until his name had been taken and he had been examined. As the doctor started for the door the inspector called him back.

"Trent, tell Mike to take all the people in the reading room up in one of the rooms on the second floor. Have them all examined. I want to find out if anyone saw any person come in here or heard any sort of a sound. Tell him to go the limit to get their stories. If they won't talk, pinch them. Somebody must have seen something during the afternoon."

When they were alone he turned to Rand. "We are going to look this room over," he said. "Then I will have White brought in. We got him as we came up the steps. He was in a hurry; felt pretty bad at seeing us. But this is not the sort of thing he would pull off. Took nerve to kill her, with all those people within sound of her voice—and nerve is not Joe's long suit."

The examination of the office revealed nothing of any value. It was true that under a heap of papers they found a hundred and fifty dollars. The sum surprised Rand a little, but the fact that it was on the desk seemed to show that robbery could not have been the motive of the crime. Though it had been placed under a heap of papers, the money could be plainly seen by anyone who had looked at the desk. As he watched the police inspector he began to grow more puzzled. That the woman should have been killed in her office was a startling thing. It was very far from being a private office. Though the librarian did not leave it often, all day long her assistants were running in and out. The office seemed to Rand to be the last place in the city for a premeditated crime. This aspect of the affair puzzled him, but to think of a motive bothered him even more. For thirty-five years the woman had been in the public library. Her disposition had grown a bit sour during the years, and people often grumbled because she was not as courteous as she should have been. But that anyone would plan her death seemed absurd. She might not have been very well liked, but he doubted that she had any real enemies.

Kent had dropped to his knees before the safe, and for a moment peered into its interior. When he rose to his feet he stood looking at the woman's body; then his glance went across the desk and his eyes narrowed. So far as Rand could see, there was nothing to cause the look; only a chair and behind the chair a bookcase.

"Rand, you knew this woman. Did she let many people come into her office?"

Rand replied that the librarian was a stickler for formality. Perhaps her long years of service at a small salary had soured her, for there was no doubt her disposition was not of the best. Few were the people that would have come into her office uninvited.

"That's what I thought," said Kent. "But look at that chair. It's right across from her body, just where it would be if someone had been sitting there talking with her. It looks as though someone she knew was in here, someone she was not suspicious of."

Rand gave the chair a studied look. It was pushed a little way out from the desk, in the position it would be in if the person who had been sitting in it had risen to leave the room. Kent was right. Whoever had been occupying that chair was someone the librarian had known. Strangers and people she did not like were not invited to her office.

"Someone she knew," came Kent's dry voice. "Someone who could rise and go around the desk and get behind her without her thinking anything was wrong. Then a hand was slammed over her mouth, the cord whipped around her neck and—"

The words died upon his lips as the door was flung violently open. They turned to see the thickset figure of the librarian rushing into the room. The round red face was flushed, the large eyes frightened. For a second he glanced at them, then looked over to the desk. As he glimpsed the body, the librarian's face went white, and he leaned against the wall for support.

The silence seemed endless. Neither Rand nor the inspector cared to say anything and the librarian was too shaken to speak.

"How—how did it—happen?" he gasped at length.

Kent briefly described how Rand had gone into the office and what he had discovered. When he had ended the librarian gave a long questioning look over the room as he slowly shook his head.

"And to think that it is perhaps my fault that she is dead."

"Your fault?" snapped out Kent.

Spicer nodded. A troubled look swept over his round face. With a quick look at the desk he turned to face the inspector.

"In a sense. She's been trying all afternoon to get into the office to see me. I have been away for a week, and got back only this noon. I found a note on my desk saying she wished to see me at once, had something very important to tell me."

As he paused for a second Rand saw a keen look sweep over the police official's face, but he did not speak.

"You know," came the anxious voice, "she was a queer woman and always did get on my nerves. I thought she simply had some complaint to make, so I put her off. There was a number of traveling men from the book houses to interview, and I sent back word that she could see me at five. But if I had only seen her at once, perhaps—"

"You don't know what she wanted?"

"No. But she sent in a page three times during the afternoon to see if I were free."

"And that was unusual?"

"Very. I have an idea that when I was chosen for this position she thought it ought to have been given to her. We did not have very much to do with each other, but all afternoon she was trying to get into my office. There was something on her mind."

Kent nodded. Slowly his eyes went over the bookcases, coming to rest on the surface of the desk. The sight of the money partly concealed by papers, caused him to take two steps and pick it up. Then he turned to Spicer.

"There was not much in here of any value," he started, but the action of the librarian was so surprising that the words died upon the inspector's lips.

There had come a sudden gasp from Spicer's lips as he darted over to the safe. Dropping down on his knees, he looked into the dark interior. It was a long look and when he rose to his feet his face expressed relief.

"Now what might that all mean?" began Kent.

"I just remembered that we have three or four very valuable books in the safe, but I see they are on the shelf, so that's all right."

There came a muffled expression from the inspector's lips. To Rand it sounded as if the police official doubted the value of any books which might be in the safe. After a look at the money in his palm Kent asked a question.

"We found this on the desk, Spicer. One hundred and fifty dollars. Now would you have any idea what it might be doing here?"

The librarian looked at the outstretched hand. In it lay a small heap of bills. Rand judged they were all tens. Spicer straightened up; a curious look swept over his face: he slowly shook his head.

"Of course it might be her own money. What it means I don't know, but Miss White, who was at the outside desk might."

He made a half motion to open the door. The inspector stopped him. Kent wanted to see the woman who had been at the other desk. He warned the librarian not to talk, then telling him to find the assistant, and to wait outside, he dismissed him. When the door closed he hastened over to the telephone and rang a number.

It was the police station he wanted, and he had the connection in a second. He ordered the fingerprint expert to be sent over to the library at once. Also, he wanted three more policemen and a stenographer. When he banged the receiver down on the hook he turned to Rand.

"It doesn't stand to reason she could be bumped off without somebody who was in the room outside knowing something. If they do we are going to find it out."

Rand was thinking of the librarian's statement.

All afternoon the reference librarian had wished to have an interview with her superior. Something must have bothered her. There was some secret she wished to disclose. Could the secret have had anything to do with her death?

He would have liked to think this over, but Kent had gone out of the room and beckoned for him to follow. As he passed through the door, he noticed that it was almost impossible to see the office door from the reference room. In only one place could anyone sitting at a table have a direct view of the office.

The reading room was deserted. Only a few moments before, it had been filled, all the chairs taken, every table occupied. Now there could be seen only a blue-uniformed policeman by the door. The people had vanished; the police had driven them out. The sight of the wide expanse of floor, the unoccupied tables and the deep silence which hung over the room depressed him. Only a few moments before it had been filled with people, now it was deserted.

Kent shuddered as he thought what they had left behind them in the office.

A sound caused him to lift his eyes. The librarian was reentering the room and by his side was a young woman, a woman who would have been very good to look at if her eyes had not been red from weeping and if she had been able to control the trembling of her body. But this she could not do, for the assistant had lost all control of her nerves.

As he saw her, Kent started across the floor, and they met beside one of the tables. Pulling out a chair, he motioned for the girl to be seated, and waited a moment for her to pull herself together. As this seemed something she could not do, the police official was forced to speak.

"Young lady," came his gruff voice, "I know you feel bad and all that, but my time is valuable. Your boss has been murdered and—"

There came a muffled cry from the girl's lips, and she rose in a frightened manner from her chair. With one hand gripping the table for support, she stared at the office door as if expecting it would open. Her lips were trembling, the blue eyes opened wide with fright. As she looked, little trembling cries escaped from her lips.

Rand saw an expression of disgust sweep over the inspector's face. He knew what the man was thinking.

Time was valuable and before them was a hysterical young woman, one who had lost all control of her nerves and would be unable to answer any questions until she had calmed down. With a gesture the inspector turned to the librarian.

"Take her somewhere and tell her I will see her in a few moments."

The girl was led from the room with the librarian's arm around her shoulders. It was not a dignified retreat, for she was letting herself go. They could hear her voice, broken with sobs, dying away in the distance. As he listened, Kent swore; swore just once, but that once was enough.

He might have spoken if two men had not come through the door. One was a young patrolman, the other, who carried a tin box under his arm, was the fingerprint expert. Reaching the inspector's side they paused. Receiving his instructions, the fingerprint expert hastened toward the office door, leaving the policeman behind.

There came another interruption. A policeman was pushing a shrinking figure into the room, a little protesting man, who swore rather loudly and did not wish to look at the inspector, a man dressed in a faded brown suit, whose feet slid over the floor far more than they walked.

As he stood before them, Joe White was not a pleasing sight. He had not shaved for several days and the rough beard gave his thin cheeks an unpleasant color. The narrow, shifting eyes shot one fleeting look at the inspector; then their gaze dropped to the floor. There was no doubt the man was ill at ease and, Rand thought, a bit frightened.

The inspector's hand fell on White's shoulders and he pulled the little figure close to him. As the captive did not look up, Kent's other hand threw White's head back. For a moment the eyes of the two men met. Then came the low, slow voice of the official:

"Well, Joe, what's it been this time?"

"Nothing," came the whining reply. "I ain't done a thing, chief. You have no right to pull me around like this."

"No?" barked out Kent. "What were you trying to sneak out of the building for?"

For a second White raised his head and Rand saw a nervous, anxious look leap into the man's eyes.

Then came the whining voice, and there was a trace of fear in the tones:

"Had a right to leave the place if I wanted. It's a public building."

Kent scowled, his eyes studying the figure before him for a moment, then he took his hand from the man's shoulder. His voice was like the barking of a machine gun.

"Joe, in that office is Ruby Merton, dead. Just been bumped off. What do you know about it?"

They saw the little figure sway for a moment; then White dropped into the nearest chair. He did not speak, neither did he raise his eyes. The thin hands were clasping each other, and his face grew pale.

When he did lift his head, the look they received was a mixture of fear and doubt. The shrill voice trembled when he spoke.

"Dead?" he gasped.

Kent nodded, waiting for a reply. There was no reply. Not until he had been asked again and again the question: "What do you know about her death?" did he speak. Then it was only to shake his head and say that he knew nothing.

But he did know something. Rand was sure of that. He remembered how he had watched White studying the office door. There had been curiosity on his face, then also anticipation. He had known something. But that Joe White had the courage to kill anyone Rand doubted.

Yet the man was afraid. It could be seen in his trembling hands; it flashed forth in his eyes. What Kent might be thinking Rand could not tell, but he was pretty sure of one thing—White had been startled when the inspector had told him the librarian was dead, not only startled but actually surprised.

Try his best, Kent could not get the man to speak. To every question he would shake his head, remain silent and motionless. This stubborn spell surprised both the inspector and Rand. There had been other occasions when the law had reached out for White.

He had always been willing to talk then. In the end, disgusted and angry, Kent's hand went slamming down on White's shoulder and he pulled the shrinking figure to its feet. For a moment the police official scowled at the man before him; then he turned to the policeman. "Take him over to the station and throw him in a cell," he ordered.

The two started over the floor, and Kent watched the tall policeman as he half pulled, half shoved his prisoner along. White knew something, but what? Then, as they had almost reached the door, Kent remembered the look in White's eyes when he ordered him to be taken to jail. It had been a look of relief.

"Jake," he called out, "bring him back."

The policeman stopped and brought his prisoner back to the inspector's side. For a second Kent looked down at the sullen figure, then reaching forth he pulled him close to his side and, with the other hand, began to search his pockets. There were several pocket knives, pencils, bits of string, a paper of tobacco and two cheap pipes. These did not interest the official, but they were all he found in the pockets. Rand had noticed that the search was far from pleasing to White, but, when Kent finished and stepped back to throw a gloomy look at the objects on the table, he saw a flash of relief sweep over White's face. It passed away when the inspector ordered the man to take off his shoes. He started to protest but Kent shoved him down into a chair and motioned to a policeman.

They were not very good shoes, or very clean. As they were pulled from his feet, White started to protest. His frightened eyes watched the long fingers of the inspector go searching into the shoes. From the look on the man's face, Rand knew that something would be found.

The first shoe revealed nothing, but when his fingers went into the toes of the second, Kent gave a little nod of satisfaction. They saw his hand come forth, noticed the quick glance he gave the object he was holding, watched the look that swept over his face.

"Well, Joe," came the cold voice, "suppose you tell us what you were doing with five ten dollar bills hidden in

the toe of your shoe? They look like companions of the
fifteen which were on Miss Merton's desk."

CHAPTER THREE

A deep silence fell over the room. The inspector stood glaring down at the shrinking figure in the chair. For the moment he did not care to speak. As for White, he would have been unable to say a word if he had wished to talk. With his face twisted into a frightened grin, the blinking eyes gazed at Kent's outstretched hand, gazed as though ten dollar bills were some strange oddity he had never seen before. "Well, Joe?" came Kent's voice again, and, though the tone was low and even, the icy edge behind the inflection caused White to jump. Unable to meet Kent's gaze he looked at the floor as he stammered out an excuse.

"I got that jack, working."

Kent gave a scornful laugh. That Joe White would ever receive fifty dollars for any sort of work was something that could not happen unless there had been a miracle. For Joe White to work would have been a miracle.

Kent's lips went suddenly tight. His hand shot out to yank White upright from the chair. With a half twist he sent the frightened man spinning into the arms of the nearest policeman.

"Joe," came the snarling word, "you talk, and you talk damn quick. Tell me where you got that money or over to the jail you go with a charge of murder against you. What's more, I'll make it stick."

White's face had grown pale and his lips twitched. Throwing out his hands in a gesture, he tried to slip from the clutching grasp which held him. Then suddenly words came tumbling from his lips.

"I never croaked her, not me, never. Don't hang that on me, chief. I did swipe the jack, but I never croaked her."

The thin face was working nervously as he pleaded with the inspector. He was deadly frightened. Rand could see that, but he doubted very much if White knew anything about the woman's death. If he had gone into the office to steal the money, it could only have been when no one was there. If he had found her dead, he never would have remained in the reading room.

What White told them seemed to prove that Rand's idea had been right. In a voice which broke as he looked into the stern face of the inspector, the captive told his story. Though the little man seemed to have become even smaller, yet there was a frightened sincerity behind his words.

He had seen Miss Merton come out of her office and go over to the desk where her assistant was sitting. Rand could see this desk; it was on the other side of the room from the private office. In a few moments the librarian had returned. White had observed that she was carrying money in her hand. Entering her office, she had remained there for a while; then she came out again. This time she went out of the reading room.

Rand could picture the sneak thief as he watched the woman leave the room. In her office was money, and for the moment the place was deserted. It was too strong a temptation and, if he told the truth, all he had done was to make a bluff of going to a magazine rack and then suddenly to dart into the little room.. The money was half hidden under a blotter, and he had taken five of the bills.

Kent had listened without a word. When White paused for breath the inspector spoke.

"You say you saw her come over from the desk over there, and that she was carrying the money in her hand, then when she went out of her office you sneaked in there?" he queried.

The eagerness with which White nodded was impressive. For a second the inspector looked at him, then, with a weary note in his voice motioned to the policeman. "Take him over to the police station and lock him up. On your way out tell them to have the librarian bring back that girl."

Protesting loudly, White was pushed out of the reading room. As he vanished through the door, the fingerprint expert came out of the office. While he crossed over to their side, Rand saw there was a pleased look on the man's face. He started to talk while some feet away. "I picked a half dozen or more prints. What else do you want done?"

Kent shook his head in a dubious fashion.

"There are at least a hundred people in the building," he said, "counting those who were in this room and the girls who work here. I guess you better make sure you stay in the station. There may be other prints I shall want you to take."

With a nod the man left them. Kent turned to gaze reflectively over the room. Now that it was empty it appeared to be a large place. He sighed as he thought of what was ahead of him. Every single person in the building would have to be examined, and there must be over a hundred. There would be little sleep tonight. Rand's voice broke in on his gloomy thoughts. "You believe White?" he queried.

"Yes," came the slow reply. "Joe would not have nerve enough to kill her. He's no killer anyway, and if he had sneaked in to that office and found her dead in her chair, you can be sure he would not have stayed around. Not he. Here comes that damned girl."

Mr. Spicer was coming across the floor. Behind him was the reluctant figure of the girl. Though her lips were trembling, yet she appeared to have gained control of her feelings to some extent. They saw her give one look at the private office, and for a second Rand thought she would make another scene, but her lips shut tight as she hurriedly glanced away. Pulling a chair from the table, Kent motioned for her to be seated. For a moment he studied her face, then spoke softly:

"You can help us a great deal if you will only answer my questions. There is nothing to be excited about. No harm can come to you."

The girl's face grew very serious as she nodded.

Though her hands were nervously clasping and unclasping, she leaned back in her chair to wait for the first question.

"You were on duty in the reading room this afternoon?"

The girl nodded.

"Did you see Miss Merton during the afternoon?"

"Three of four times."

"When was the last time?"

"I should say a little before four o'clock. She came to my desk to get the money from the Women's Club."

The look she received caused her to add quickly:

"It was money given by the Women's Club for a memorial picture to be hung in one of the branch libraries."

She had gained control of her nerves and her voice had become stronger. In reply to the inspector's questions, she informed him that the amount was two hundred dollars. Twenty ten dollar bills had been given to her superior, who had taken them to her private office. A few moments later she had seen Miss Merton going out of the reference room. The inspector gave a glance at his wrist watch as a scowl swept over his face. Time was passing and they were getting nowhere. All that had been discovered, Rand could have written in one sentence, and it would have been a short one at that. The next question was very direct:

"Do you know if Miss Merton had any visitors in her office this afternoon?"

"Three. A book salesman was in around two, and stayed until two-thirty. At three Professor Henry Harlen went in the office. He stayed until—oh, perhaps thirty minutes. And one of the girls was in there after the professor."

Rand knew what was passing through Kent's mind. Three people had been in the private office and, though what they would have to say would be of little value, it would prove one thing. Up until about four the woman was still alive. Could anyone have gone into the office and not been observed by the assistant in the reading room? After all, her desk was in such a position that she would have been unable to see the office door.

To Rand's surprise, Kent did not pursue this line of information. Instead, after one look at the girl, he wanted to know if she had observed anything out of the way in the dead woman's manner during the day. A shrewd expression swept over the girl's face.

She cast a doubtful look at the floor, then raised her eyes. The look was a keen one, filled with a little trace of excitement. Now that her hysteria had passed, the reporter could see that she was not only a very pretty girl but also a rather intelligent one. When she replied there was a half apologetic tone in her voice: "It may mean nothing, sir, but she was very much excited all day. Again and again during the morning she tried to get some number on the telephone. I think she must have gotten her party about one o'clock, for she did not use the phone after that. I thought that she was not only excited but also, perhaps, a little shocked."

"You have no idea whom she wanted, whom she was trying to get on the telephone?"

The girl shook her head. The reference librarian had a direct line outside the building and, as the telephone system was automatic, the calls could not be traced through the exchange. But the woman had tried again and again to get a number, the girl was sure of this, for during the morning she had been working at a table just outside the office door. She had heard the telephone being used.

The inspector was silent a moment, then with a wave of his hand motioned the girl to go. She had taken but one step toward the door, however, when he called her back.

"I noticed that there is another door in her office. I presume that it leads out to a hallway. Did she keep that door locked?"

"Always. You see—" the girl hesitated a moment giving Spicer a half glance, but the look upon Kent's face caused her to say what was on her mind. "You see, she hated to have people running in to see her. So she locked that door, always kept it locked. I know it was locked around two-thirty, for one of the girls told me she was bringing a book to Miss Merton and tried the hallway door. It was locked."

Whatever Kent thought of her reply could not be told from his face. With a grunt he told the girl he would not want her any longer and at the same time asked Spicer to see that all his assistants were gathered in one room. The man hurried away, and Kent stood for a moment in a brown study. Then, with a sudden shrug of his shoulders, he turned to Rand.

"Rand," he said, "I have to go upstairs and see if my men have picked up anything from that gang they have herded together. We are not getting anywhere. While I am upstairs suppose you go and see if that office door is locked. You might hang around here till the body is moved. I will give you what dope I get later."

Rand walked over the floor, hesitating a second before the closed office door. Straightening up his shoulders he pushed it open and entered the room. He tried not to give a glance at the still figure at the desk, but was unable to turn his eyes away. The glance was only for a second, however; the next instant he was standing before the door which was opposite the one he had just pushed open.

It was a wooden door, and there was a key in the
lock, but when he turned the knob the door swung open.
The girl had said that Miss Merton always kept the door
locked; what was more, one of her assistants had tried
the door earlier in the afternoon. It was locked then. It
was now unlocked.

Pushing the door open, he stepped out into a small
hallway. To his left was another door, its top glass. He
could see part of the large lounge, though the view was
broken by high pillars. To his right the hall ran only
about six feet, and there was a door which he thought
opened into the basement.

He stood there for a while thinking. If the door was
always locked, if it had been locked at three, then the
murderer had simply turned the key and escaped through
the hallway. It would be an easy thing to do. Though he
might be observed as he stepped into the lounge, yet
again he might not be. Anyone who was careful and
picked the moment well, could dart to one of the pillars
and be unseen.

When he stepped back into the office, for some
unknown reason, he turned the key in the lock. He gave it
a moody glance, then stepped over to the desk and sank
down into the chair. One hand reached out for the
telephone. While he had the time, he had better phone
into the rewrite man what he had found. But just as he
was about to dial the number he gave a start.

For some reason the desk did not look natural. Why
he thought this he did not know, but there was something
that should have been on the table, which was not there.
It was not the money that had been under the blotter, for
the inspector had taken that. So far as he could see,
nothing had been disturbed, and yet—

Slowly his eyes searched every section of the desk. He
noticed the pile of magazines, the copies of the Publishers'
Weekly, the orderly row of book catalogues. For a second
he even allowed his eyes to rest upon that white head, a
head sunk down upon a still chest. Everything seemed to

be as it was when he first came into the office. But he knew that something was missing. Again his eyes started to travel over the desk; then suddenly he gave a start. There was one thing missing. The inspector had not taken it, and the finger-print expert would touch nothing. But one thing was gone. He had watched the inspector examine the cord which had been around the woman's neck. After one look Kent had tossed it upon the desk. It had been upon the desk when they left the office to go into the reading room, but it was not there now. Nowhere in the room could he see that bit of cord.

CHAPTER FOUR

Leaning back in the chair, Rand stared at the desk as though he had never seen it before. When he rose to his feet, he lifted each book, picked up every piece of paper. After examining the desk, he searched the rest of the room, and in the end he was forced to admit that the bit of cord had vanished.

Kent had not placed it in his pocket; he was positive of that. The inspector had thrown the cord on the desk and had not picked it up again. Spicer had seen the cord but had not touched it. The fingerprint expert had not touched it Rand was sure; he certainly would not have taken it from the room. However, it was gone.

Rand's eyes rested upon the door which opened into the hallway. He gave a start. The bit of cord was missing, and none of the police had taken it, but someone might have come into the office from the hallway. If this had happened, the cord had been taken while Kent and Rand were out in the reading room. He thought of this for a moment, as a shrewd look swept over his face. That bit of cord had been the weapon by which the librarian had been killed. It was of no interest to anyone save the murderer. Then he gave a little whistle.

Whoever had taken the cord must still be in the building. The inspector had stated that he had policemen at all the doors, and that no one was allowed to enter or leave the building until he had been examined. There had been no time as yet to examine anyone.

Whoever had taken the string must still be in the building.

His first idea was to rush from the room and tell the inspector, but by this time Kent would be on the second floor trying to discover what the people who had been in the reading room had observed. Then he had another idea.

Going into the hallway he turned to his left. He paused by the door that led to the lobby and glanced through the glass. Leaning against the post was a uniformed policeman. Rand gave the thickset figure one glance then pushed open the door and called out. With a slight start of surprise, the man turned around and gazed at the reporter. At the sight of Rand's beckoning finger he came slowly across the floor. Every policeman in the city knew the reporter, and a half grin passed over the officer's face as he reached Rand's side.

"Have you seen anyone come through this door?" Rand questioned quickly.

The policeman slowly shook his head.

"No." was the very positive reply. Seeing that one word was not enough, he went into details. "I have been back of that post for the last thirty minutes. There is a man outside. My job is to see that no one sneaks out. There ain't been no one past me, and if they tried to come past that door I would see them. What you want to know for?"

There was an interested look upon the policeman's face; he was willing to listen. With a little shake of his head Rand murmured some excuse and stepped back into the hallway. As the door closed he stood silent a moment. One thing seemed sure; no one had gone out into the lobby. It would have been impossible to do so without being seen by the watching policeman.

But there was another door in the hallway, and he judged that it went down into the basement. Whoever had taken the cord had to come through the hallway door. Then the basement must be the place where the murderer had vanished.

Walking to the end of the passage, he threw the door open and found himself looking down into a pit of blackness. It was after six o'clock and, because of the storm, darkness had already fallen over the city.

The cellar into which he was looking no doubt passed under the entire building. Just how large it was he did not know.

Passing through the doorway, he went down two steps and then stood listening. Not a sound came to his ears, but after a moment he could make out the windows across the floor. High up in the wall were two dim squares not quite so black as the rest of the cellar.

To go down in the dark cellar, not knowing its size or what it might contain, did not seem a very sensible thing to do. There must be a switch somewhere, and he turned to see if it was on the wall behind him. Not finding it, he decided that it must be at the bottom of the steps.

There were just seven steps but when he stood on the concrete cellar floor he found that the cellar was even darker than he had thought. True, across the floor he could make out the two small windows, but they were only a trifle lighter than the cellar itself. A hand went searching in his pocket for his lighter and finding it he flipped the spring, but though there came a tiny spark the wick did not ignite. As he thrust the trinket back into his pocket he remembered that he had been intending to fill it all day. He would have to depend upon matches if he wished a light. Matches were one thing Carty Rand was never able to keep in his pockets. When he had made a careful search, he held just five in his hand. They ought to be enough, for all he wished was to discover the switch for the electric lights. It must be on the wall by his side.

He struck a match, and as the flicker of flame leaped into being quickly looked about him. High on the wall was the switch; just as the match went spluttering out, his fingers touched the button. But though he turned it over, the cellar did not leap forth into light.

Again and again his nervous fingers tugged and snapped the switch, but to no avail. Either the lights were turned off in the cellar or there was something wrong. He had found the switch but he could get no illumination. The thing would not work.

With his back pressed against the wall he peered out into the darkness. Like a huge tunnel of gloom, the cellar stretched away before him. In the blackness it had neither shape nor size, seemingly stretching away into chaos—a sinister darkness, he thought, which threatened to engulf him if he moved.

Just what to do he did not know. Two floors above, Kent would be examining the library patrons, trying to find some fact which might throw light on the crime. He knew what Kent would say when told of the disappearance of the cord, could see his face flush with eagerness. Perhaps the best thing to do was to go back up the steps.

Yet he hesitated. The cord had vanished. Whoever had taken it must have come down into the cellar. He knew there must be another entrance to the basement; no doubt it was at the other end of the building. If he went to the center of the floor, and picked his way carefully, he ought to be able to find it.

Suddenly there came over him the feeling that he was not alone. Though he could see nothing, and no sound drifted to his ears, yet a little shiver swept over him. It was an indescribable feeling, as though a sudden cold wind passed through the basement.

As he felt it he realized that he was not alone.

Pressed close against the wall he bent forward and listened. For a moment he heard nothing. Then he thought he could hear the rain hitting against the windows, but the sound was so faint he could barely hear it.

He tried to throw his nervousness aside, telling himself that it was caused by the darkness and silence, but he knew that he was simply deceiving himself. Someone was in the cellar; though he could neither see nor hear the person, yet he knew someone was there. The very air he breathed seemed filled with a threatening presence. Again the shiver passed over him and he gave one look at the steps. They were overhead, but so dense was the gloom that it was rather difficult to make out the shadowy outline. It was then that he was sure he heard a sound.

It was not much of a sound, yet it could not be mistaken. A little to his right had come a curious scraping on the cement floor, the dragging sound of creeping coming in his direction, feet which were trying to pick their way without a noise.

He had courage enough, but his heart took a sudden pounding leap. Whoever was in the cellar knew he was there, must have seen him come down the steps, caught the flare of his match. Now this unknown was stalking him in the darkness.

The sound had come from the direction of the stairway. Rand tried to pierce the darkness with his glance, but could see nothing. As he pressed against the wall, he thought he heard someone breathe. Then he gave one leap in the direction of the stairway.

As he leaped away from the wall he slammed into the unseen body of a man. His hand brushed against a shoulder; his face felt the rough cloth as it scraped against his cheek. Then a hand came clutching down upon his shoulder.

With a burst of strength he threw it off, only to feel it clutching at his coat. A fist crashed against his arm. Though it was only a slanting blow, yet the force sent him backward. As he half stumbled, his unseen assailant came rushing after him.

As they clinched, Rand knew that it would take all his skill and strength to keep on his feet, but keep his feet he must, for his opponent was larger and heavier than himself. Once down on the concrete he would be at a disadvantage. He must keep his feet as long as he could.

A hand was creeping over his shoulder, searching for his throat. Rand felt long sinuous fingers clutching at his flesh. Desperately he threw them off and sent his fist against the man's chest. The blow drove him back, but only for a second. The next he had rushed in again.

As they struggled back and forth in the darkness, for some unknown reason Rand did not call out. He could hear the heavy breathing of his opponent, feel the hands which clutched and tore at his clothing, but neither of them spoke.

Once the man's arms encircled Rand's waist, and he was almost thrown to the floor. Shaking himself loose, he reached out his hand, only to have his fingers entangled in the pocket of a coat. As they slipped in they clutched something, which, as he drew away, he kept securely in his hand.

Leaping back he thrust the object into his pocket as the man rushed him against the side of the stairway. Struggling to break away, he felt the pressure of the strong hands upon his arms, sensed the cutting edge of the stairway. Here he was at a disadvantage, and he realized to his horror that the man had a grip which he could not break.

The side of the stair was cutting into his back; the pressure was getting stronger, and he felt a sudden twinge of pain. A hand crept up his arm, slid over his shoulder, then the long fingers fixed around his throat.

He shook one arm away, and struck out wildly with his clenched fist. He felt it go smashing upon the man's throat and realized that the grip around his neck had been broken. He gave a leap for the steps, leaped again as the man jumped forward to catch him, and managed to escape the grasp.

His feet reached the first step then the second. Half creeping, half climbing, he dragged himself toward the open door, and knew that the danger was over. The man had given up the idea of following him. He heard footsteps running over the cellar floor, heard them die away as, with a gasp, he staggered through the door into the hallway.

The first instinctive action was to lean wearily against the wall. Next he closed the door and turned the key which was in it. His wind was gone and he was panting. By the light which came from the lobby he saw that his clothes were in a sorry state. For several moments he leaned against the wall. Just what the episode in the cellar might mean he did not at the moment try to fathom. His entire body ached, and where the man's fingers had encircled his throat there was a fiery pain.

As his strength came flooding back, he realized that he must get to Kent at once. The man must still be in the cellar, unless he had managed to escape through the windows. Rand knew he must hurry to Kent and have the cellar searched at once.

Suddenly he remembered the object his fingers had clutched when they slipped into the man's pocket. He found the object and for a moment his fingers rested on it. When his hand came out into the light he gave a long look at the thing clutched in his fingers. It was a sober look and at the same time a wondering one. There in his hand was a piece of cord, a harmless looking bit of cord, to look at, but Rand knew that it was not as harmless as it appeared, for in his hand he was holding the cord which had been around the librarian's throat.

CHAPTER FIVE

Only for a second did he look at the cord. Thrusting it back into his pocket he turned and started for the lobby. The policeman, still standing beside the first pillar, gave him a friendly glance as he hurried by, but Rand did not even nod.

Rushing up a wide stairway he came out on the balcony which ran around the large court. To his right were the art gallery and the special library, and across the court was a lecture room. Both art gallery and lecture room contained people, and after a quick glance he saw that Kent was in the special library.

He paused by the door and looked into the room. In front of a book-lined wall, the tall inspector was seated at a desk. Beside him sat a stenographer and behind her was a policeman. A worried looking man was answering the questions which were being hurled at him.

It was several moments before the inspector looked in the direction of the door. A scowl swept over his face as Rand beckoned and for a moment Rand thought he would not leave the desk, but at last he rose and hastened out into the hallway.

"It's no time to ask me any questions," he growled.

"Listen to what I am going to spill," was the retort.

In a few words the trip to the cellar and the fight were described. As Kent's eyes opened in astonishment, Rand took from his pocket the piece of black cord. With a shrug of his shoulders he placed it in the inspector's outstretched palm.

Turning it over and over in his big hands, Kent's eyes searched every inch of the string.

"It's the same cord," he growled as he turned to the policeman who was in the book-lined room.

"Come here, Hank," he commanded.

Short and vivid were the orders the man received. He was to take another officer and search the cellar from one end to the other. If they found anyone there they were to bring him up to the second floor.

As the man started to leave Kent growled out that if he had to shoot, then shoot.

Rand followed the officer to the first floor. There was little interest in listening to a hundred people being asked the same questions. That the man was still in the cellar he doubted. Nor was he surprised when, after the end of their thirty-minute search, nothing had been found.

It had been a careful search. Every inch of the cellar had been looked over. Packing cases had been moved, piles of old magazines disturbed. Under the light from the flashlights the remotest corners had been looked into. Even the dark furnace room had been searched, and two tons of coal had been disturbed. But there were no signs of anyone.

It was not until they began to look at the windows that they found one was open. A packing case stood below it, and the dust upon the sill showed that someone had crawled through. There was no doubt the man had left the cellar.

Rand crawled slowly back to the second floor and again looked through the door. Kent was still at the table and a look into the art gallery showed there were at least thirty persons yet to be examined. As the inspector turned to glance in his direction Rand shook his head, only to have his gesture repeated by Kent.

Digging into a pocket he found a loose cigarette and slowly lighted it. He knew what Kent's shake of the head meant. Nothing had been discovered from the persons who were passing before the desk. He had an idea nothing would be discovered. With a half sigh he glanced at his wrist watch, scowling when he saw the time.

It was after seven. By all rights he should be at the paper, for his chief had said he would wait at the office for him. It would be several hours before the inspector would be through with his examinations. Rand decided to go to the office and send a cub back in case anything should break while he was away.

As he slipped out of the building and felt the rain dashing over his hot face he realized that he was a little tired. Night had fallen and with the coming of darkness the storm had increased. The wind was howling across the river, hurling the rain in blinding sheets over the pavement. Upon the flagpole in front of the library, the flag, which should have been pulled down at sundown, was being whipped to shreds by the wind.

He was lucky enough to find a taxi across the street and after giving the address, he sank down on the seat with a sigh of relief. Lighting another cigarette, he started to run over in his mind the story he would write. He was still thinking of it when they stopped before the Star building. The Star filled a unique position in newspaper circles. It was the only newspaper in a city of a quarter of a million, and had both a morning and an evening edition. Rand did not have to fear being scooped by other reporters, but when he reached the fourth floor, and went into the office of the city editor, he was surprised to find the big boss himself sitting behind a desk.

He gave his story, was asked a few questions, then was told to write what he had discovered and stick to the case. There was a twinkle in the editor's eyes when he asked Rand if he wanted another man to help him out. The reporter's hasty refusal caused the editor to laugh.

It was nine o'clock when Carty Rand came out of the restaurant next door to the Star building and hailed a taxi. Giving the police station as an address, he climbed in and put his legs up on the other seat. He had written his story, had something to eat and was now set for the night.

As they drove through the rain-swept streets, he wondered if Kent had finished examining the people who had been in the library. That they would know anything he doubted, yet there had been fifty persons in that reading room, some one of them must have seen something.

At the police station he went at once to the office of the homicide squad and pushed open the glass door. Though the lights were on, no one was behind the desk. A sergeant stuck his head through the door and said that the inspector was just leaving the library. Also, he had asked that some supper be sent into his office.

When the tall figure came through the door, Rand needed but one look at the official's face to tell that nothing new had been discovered. There was a weary expression upon Kent's face, a perplexed look in his eyes. With a sigh he sank down in his chair and slowly packed a much worn pipe. Before he could strike the match, a messenger boy came into the room bearing a covered basket, from which the boy produced a plate of thin sandwiches, a thermos bottle filled with coffee, and two pieces of rather sorry looking pie. As a supper it was not much, but it seemed to satisfy the inspector. When the last crumb of the pie had vanished, Kent lighted his pipe and threw a long reflective look at the reporter.

"We know no more than we did when you called me over," was the dry comment. Then, after the pipe was drawing to suit him, he shook his head and added, "But Joe White can't be the boy."

One of the patrons of the library had seen White slip into the office. This witness was positive that the librarian had left the reading room and that, when she did, White had risen from his chair and entered the office. He was there only a moment and it was some time after he had taken his seat that the woman had returned to the room.

"That let's Joe out. At that I never thought he had nerve enough to commit a murder."

That Kent was worried was apparent. Angry, quick puffs of smoke were coming from his mouth, around which was a tight line, and he scowled at Rand as though expecting him to speak and throw some light upon the crime. Seeing the look, the reporter asked one question:

"What about the bit of cord that was taken from the office?"

"That string may prove to be the only clue we have. It's a good hunch the bird who sneaked back to get it was the murderer. He must have been in the building all the time. What's more he was afraid to leave the cord there."

This was a little too much for Rand. Sarcastically he inquired if the inspector thought the murderer had waited around the building until the body had been discovered and the string placed on the desk.

To his surprise that was just about what Kent did mean.

Placing his pipe on the edge of the desk, the official grew serious. In his opinion, the murderer had realized that it was a question of only a few moments before the crime would be discovered. He wanted the string, because he was afraid it might be traced. Rand gave a scornful laugh.

"Trace a bit of strong cord?" he queried.

"Sure, when the cord is the kind it is. Not so many people of the city would have that sort of string with them. It's the sort of thing you find on fishing boats."

Though the cord had been in his possession and he had looked at it several times, it had suggested nothing to Rand. Now he repeated Kent's words:

"It's the sort of thing you find on fishing boats."

The thought of his stupidity was not pleasing. Kent was right. It might be possible to trace the cord. For a while they talked of the motive. The police had failed to find any reason for the woman's death, and even to think of one seemed beyond their imagination. A hundred and fifty dollars was on the desk—it had not been touched.

Robbery was not the motive, and the woman had no real enemies.

Rand was informed that though every person in the library had been interviewed, their testimony was of no value. Not one individual had heard or seen anything out of the way. Even the man who had noticed White slip into the private office had not thought anything of the action.

There were thirty-one individuals on the library staff and all but two of them were women. Not one had the slightest fact which would throw any light on the crime. As he said this the inspector shook a very gloomy head.

But Rand was not so certain the official was right. He knew Kent and had a great deal of admiration for his ability, but, after all, the inspector was an unimaginative man, trained in the old-fashioned methods of police work. That meant that certain things were done as a matter of course. Witnesses were examined, fingerprints taken, such clues as could be observed, run down.

But in this affair, the usual detail work had run into a blind alley. There were no clues to be examined, the persons who should have been witnesses knew nothing, and there was little doubt that they had told the truth. As for the fingerprints, the inspector had just said, there was not likely to be any help there. True, all the persons in the library had been fingerprinted, and later there would be a report, but Kent had no hopes in that direction. Rand felt there was one thing overlooked. The assistant librarian had said that her superior had been excited and nervous all day. During the morning she had tried again and again to get a telephone number. She had wanted to see the librarian, and several times had sent in to see if she could have an interview. It was Rand's opinion that if Spicer had seen her when he first came into the building there would have been no murder.

Voicing these opinions, he had the satisfaction of having Kent listen, though his face did not change in expression. When Rand ran out of words, there came the inspector's curt query:

"It's all so, but what do you make out of it?"

Rand threw his cigarette into an ash tray and rose slowly to his feet. He was a tall young man whose body could stand at least twenty more pounds. As he gazed down at the slouched figure of Kent a little gleam of excitement flashed into his gray eyes.

"Nothing, Kent. But I know this. Ruby Merton was an emotional old soul. She was always excited about something. But we heard today that she was very much excited. First she tried to see Spicer. Why that bird did not see her when he first got her note is a thing he may regret. But something bothered her. Maybe she discovered something when she came down to her office."

The figure in the chair straightened up to cast one look at Rand. Seeing the question upon his face the reporter threw out his hands in a helpless gesture.

"God knows what it might be, but there was something which scared and bothered her. She knew something. It's a good hunch the murderer killed her to keep her mouth shut." Kent puffed away silently and Rand added a question: "Kent, who is in the library?"

"I left Blake on duty. Thought I'd better keep someone in the building all night. Why?"

"Why?" came the retort. "Just this, Kent. The entire answer to this murder must be in that library. Whatever it was got the old lady disturbed, it happened right there in the building. If I could stumble upon what it was, then we could get somewhere."

Kent gave him a serious look. There was a good deal of sense in what he said. It was no ordinary murder, one which could be solved by the usual hit and miss method. Until he had some idea as to the motive behind the crime, he could not get very far. Rand was a pretty shrewd reporter; he might stumble upon something.

Dropping down into the chair he wrote out an order. When he rose to place it in the outstretched hand he uttered a word of warning: "Give this to Blake, but if you find anything, call me up."

CHAPTER SIX

A VERY pleased policeman opened the library door. His pleasure was due to the reporter's saying that for the next hour he would not be alone. That he was to have company caused a wide smile to break across Blake's face. The deserted building had been getting on his nerves, and the gloomy sound of the rain dashing against the many windows had been far from pleasing.

Rand could tell that the policeman was not enjoying his assignment. Lights were on in the lobby and the reference room was not dark. Even the long rows of stacks behind the delivery desk were illumined by lights in each aisle. Blake had evidently decided that if he had to be alone in the building, at least he would not be in the dark.

Telling him he wished to be alone in the private office, Rand went into the reading room. Because it was unoccupied, it seemed much larger than usual. As he crossed the floor, the orderly rows of chairs at the vacant tables reminded him of the scene in the late afternoon. Then the room had been filled.

With the policeman at his heels, he paused by the door which opened into the private office. For a second the thought came to him that he was doing an absurd thing. Kent had examined the room and found nothing. That he could succeed where the police had failed seemed doubtful. Yet he felt certain that the office held the solution of the crime. Pushing open the door he found the switch and turned on the light. As the room leaped into vision, instinctively he threw a glance at the desk. But the chair which had contained the body was now empty.

He knew the policeman was wondering what he was doing in the building, so he turned and said that he wished to examine the room. With a shrug of his shoulders, the officer replied that he would look over a magazine, and, digging into a pocket, brought forth a pipe. Lighting it, he ambled away in the direction of the magazine racks.

Sinking into a chair, Rand lighted a cigarette and began to study the little room. Across from him was the green safe, the doors still open. Around the walls were the bookcases, their shelves crowded with magazines and reference works. The desk seemed undisturbed, except that the money, which had been half hidden under a paper, was no longer there.

The more he glanced around the room the more puzzled he became. It was an incredible sort of a crime. That anyone in the city should have murdered Ruby Merton was beyond belief. That the murder should have taken place in a building filled with people seemed impossible.

Lighting another cigarette, he decided to start at the beginning. What could be the motive? The more he thought this over, the more puzzled he became. The woman had been a public servant, without either enemies or friends. Revenge, passion, theft, all the things which may enter into the usual crime could not have applied to her death. Yet there had been a motive, and the murderer must have been desperate, so desperate that he had taken the chance of being detected. Why? Then he began to remember what the assistant had said.

From the time she came into her office the woman had been excited. All morning long she had tried to get someone on the telephone. Then there was her attempt to see the librarian. If Spicer had not put the woman off, no doubt she would still be alive. What had she wanted to tell him? What had she discovered?

He thought of this for a while. When she came into her office she had made some discovery. Then he gave a start. Had her telephone calls been attempts to have the murderer come down to her office? They had been told that she failed to get the party she was calling, and the assistant did not know who it was. In the end he reached a conclusion. Not only had Ruby Merton made a discovery that morning, but it had been made in her own office. What was more it had been of such importance that the individual it concerned had killed her, rather than have it made public.

If this reasoning was correct, then, some time during the day, the murderer had become informed of what the woman knew. She had been murdered in order to stop her tongue. But he wondered a little. It hardly seemed credible that any discovery she might make in the little room would be of great importance.

His glance fell upon the door which led to the hallway. There was no doubt the murderer had come through the door. This raised another question. That door was always locked, and they had been told that around three one of the girls had come down the hall and had tried the door. It had been locked then.

With a sudden shrug of his shoulders, he rose to his feet, and stood staring at the safe. If the library door had been locked, then the murderer must have entered the office from the reading room. Perhaps Kent had discovered a witness, who, while seated at a table, had seen someone go into the office. If he had, the inspector had kept the information from him.

He was half decided that it was foolish to spend any more time there. There was nothing in the office not the slightest thing which could aid him. Turning, he started for the door, but before reaching it paused. He might take a look at the safe.

It stood between two windows, its steel doors partly open. Getting down on his knees, he peered into the gloomy interior. There were the usual compartments, but there was one difference from the usual safe. One half the space was divided into shelves which were filled with books.

The compartment drawers were locked, and when he discovered this he laughed. After all, if they had been open he would have found nothing of value. He started to rise to his feet, but dropped down on his knees again. It was a good time to look over the books.

If he had one complex which stood out above all others, it was his love for books. Hours of his spare time were spent in reading. Everything written about books thrilled his soul, and his mind was filled with a store of what he often thought was useless knowledge.

There were about twenty books on the narrow shelves. They were the rare editions which the library owned, and, because they were valuable, they were not placed in general circulation. Few people had ever seen them.

Reaching into the safe, he pulled out the first books his hands fell upon, and for a few moments turned the pages. He found a first edition of Keats, four Conrads, which he knew were mounting in value, and three Hardy first editions.

There were four shelves in the safe, and he started at the first. When he reached the last one, he pulled forth five items. They had been placed in slip covers, and were small pamphlets, very old, and yet in a rather remarkable state of preservation.

The first one which he took from its case contained but seventy-two pages. He glanced at the title with a little awe, for he knew it was very valuable—"A Relation of Journal of the Beginning and Proceedings of the English Plantation settled in Plymouth"—began the very long title.

It was the very famous Mounts Relation. Many collectors called those seventy-two pages the rarest of all New England books. It contained the first printed account of the Pilgrim fathers, and was written by John Bradford. Not only was it rare, but he knew that, at the last auction sale, it had brought a price of thirty-five hundred dollars. And the library owned two copies.

He gave the pamphlet a glance, then picked up the next one. This was much smaller than the first though almost as rare. John Davenport's "Discourses about Civil Government." It had been printed in England in 1663. Over a year ago it had sold for sixteen hundred dollars. Leaning against the safe, Rand let his thoughts wander. Like all book collectors, he wondered if he would ever, say in some old dusty box, discover the rare items he had glanced at—just a few faded pages of paper, covered with old yellow letters, yet worth hundreds of dollars.

Slipping to the floor, the pamphlets lying in his lap, Rand allowed his thoughts to wander. For the time being he had forgotten what had taken place in the little room, forgotten what he had discovered in the chair by his side. His imagination was running wild.

There were five thin pamphlets in his lap. How much had happened since John Bradford first set down his quaint story of the Pilgrim fathers. Millions of men had been born, suffered, loved and died since those few sheets of paper had been covered with black letters. They were worth a great deal now, some day they would be worth a fortune.

With a little sigh of envy he bent forward to thrust them back into the safe. Closing the steel safe he stood for a moment looking down at it. It ought to be locked. No doubt in the excitement of the afternoon this had been overlooked. For a second he wondered if he should turn the dial of the combination, but decided that it was better to leave things just as he had found them.

Lighting a fresh cigarette he stood silent a moment, then walked over to the door and looked out into the reference room. Though Blake had turned on all the lights on the lower floor, yet the long empty room seemed very desolate and lonely. To shut out the sight, he closed the door, and walked back to sit in the chair by the desk.

Slumped far down in his chair, he tried to recall how the rare, early Americana had come into the possession of the library. Public libraries of small cities did not as a rule collect valuable books. Yet the five pamphlets in the safe were worth at least ten thousand dollars, perhaps more.

In the end it came to him. A wealthy resident of the city had given them to the library. There had been a clause in the will which said that they could not be sold until ten years had elapsed. That was nine years ago, and a year must pass before the library placed them on sale.

For a while his mind played with various conflicting theories. Then a question began to frame itself: Suppose the librarian had invited someone to her office that afternoon. Perhaps this was a wild idea, for to save his life he could not think of any reason why it should be done. But suppose she had, someone whom no individual in the crowded room had seen go into her office.

The thought seemed absurd, for there had been no hint of this, yet all morning long she had been trying to reach someone on the phone. Tried again and again. Whom had she been trying to reach, why had she been so determined to get her party, and for what reason?

Across from him stood the desk telephone, he gave it a somber glance. If inanimate things could only speak once in a while, how much more simple life would be. But she had failed to get her party, though she had tried again and again.

Rising, he crossed over to study the telephone. There was a little switch on the side of the desk. A smile crossed his lips as he noticed it. They had been told that Ruby Merton's telephone Was a direct line outside the building. That was true, but the switch showed that she could change over to the library exchange if she so desired.

He knew most of the girls in the building, so, dropping down in the chair, he rapidly dialed a number. When the voice came over the wire, he asked a question. Who had been on the library switchboard that day? He was given two names, one for the morning, the other for the afternoon. Leav-ing a very astonished girl at the other end of the wire, he rang off without a word of thanks.

The young woman who answered his second call assured him that she had been at the switchboard until noon. To his inquiry if Ruby Merton had made any calls outside the building, she answered "No," and added the information that, as she had a private line, she rarely made any calls through the library exchange.

Replacing the receiver, he wondered if it would be worth while to call the other girl. She had been on duty during the afternoon, and there was no doubt she would make the same reply, but because he was a good reporter he dialed the number.

To his first question she answered that she had been on duty all afternoon. He could tell from the inflection of her voice that the girl was wondering why he desired the information.

"Did Ruby Merton make any outside calls during the afternoon?"

The answer surprised him. The girl said that she had, adding that the outside connection in the office of the reading room had been out of order all morning. Miss Merton, when she had called for a number before one o'clock, had informed the girl that she had just discovered her outside line was out of order.

"Do you know whom she called?"

"She tried only two numbers," came the reply. "The first one she called not only by the number, but gave the man's name. It was Judge Allen; and he was out of town. The second one was a number only, but what it was I do not remember; she did not get her party."

Thanking her, he hung up the receiver, then cast a scowling glance at the dripping window. The information he had received was of no value. Judge Allen was out of the city, but then the Judge would know nothing of the murder anyway. He was almost the best liked man in the city. There was that other call, the uncompleted one.

With a shrug of his shoulders, he concluded that one fact at least was true. All morning she had tried to get into communication with someone, tried again and again, only to discover around one o'clock that her line had been out of order. When she put her call through the library exchange, about one o'clock, she failed to get her party.

An idea struck him. At one o'clock she would go out to lunch. She might have reached the party she wished at that time. No doubt she had tried to do so, perhaps succeeded. But why this keen desire to talk with the unknown individual?

He had known Ruby Merton well, a funny, repressed neurotic, whom life had soured, who, to say the least, was not well liked. It was also true that there were very few people whom she called friends.

It seemed probable that, if she had spent a good part of a morning trying to reach someone on the telephone, she must have been angry. He broke off his thoughts to light another cigarette. As he blew a smoke ring across the room, his eyes fell upon the door leading into the hall, a door open several inches, in whose lock he could see the key.

Here was another problem. The murderer' must have entered through that door, yet around four o'clock the door had been locked—and locked on the inside. Who had unlocked it? He wished he could answer that question.

Ruby Merton might have unlocked the door. If she had, was it because someone was coming to see her, someone whom she did not care to have come through the reference room?

This was possible. Somebody had unlocked the door, and he knew Ruby Merton well enough to feel sure that no one would touch her door while she was in the office. People took no liberties with her belongings.

Leaning back into the chair, he gave a long sigh. Suddenly he felt very weary and wondered why he had returned to the library. The visit had been of no importance; he knew no more than before he had returned to the building. He would go back to the paper, write out a short report, then go to bed.

But, for the moment, he relaxed. Then, suddenly, there came sweeping over him a great wave of loneliness. The building seemed to become very large, a desolate and empty place. It was very still. Only the rain dashing against the window broke the strange silence.

He was not a very imaginative young man, yet he felt uneasy. It was an odd uneasiness, impelling him to rise and rush from the little room, out of the silent building. What caused the feeling he could not tell, but as it again passed over him he rose to his feet. Just as he stood upright, the lights in the reference room suddenly went out.

One moment the room beyond the little office had been a blaze of light, the next it had become a pit of darkness. The square glass of the door was now a black outline, a sinister darkness he thought. As he stood staring at the glass, he caught himself listening— listening with every nerve tense.

He heard nothing and after a moment gave a faint smile. The lights had gone out in the reference room, but the bulbs in the office were on. Turning, he reached his hand down to the desk for his hat; as he picked it up, his eyes fell upon the safe. It was a dark green safe, not very large, not more than five feet high. As he glanced at it a scowl came between his eyes. That door was unlocked, inside was over ten thousand dollars' worth of rare books. The safe ought to be locked, but, after all, it was not his affair. That the door was unlocked was of course an oversight. In the excitement it had been overlooked. As he thought this, he decided he would lock it himself.

Crossing the floor he knelt and made certain that the door was closed; then his hand reached for the dial, and he heard a faint clicking sound as it locked. With one hand on the knob he was on the verge of rising to his feet when a sound caused him to become tense.

It was only a faint sound and for a second he thought it must be the rain against the window, but almost as soon as he thought this he knew he was wrong. No rain could make that sound, that soft sinister dragging noise which seemed to be behind him. With a start he made an effort to rise to his feet, began a motion which would have turned him around. Then came the blow, and pain, trickling like a white-hot iron, went searing through his brain. He felt himself sinking, sinking down into a soft darkness, a great pit of blackness, which rose to meet him; then the darkness wrapped itself around him, something seemed to explode in his brain and after that he knew no more.

CHAPTER SEVEN

As the buzzer upon his desk broke into a shrill clatter, Inspector George Kent gave a sudden nervous start. It was an insistent, determined ring, and it seemed to him a bit angry. He knew who was responsible for the sound. In his private office Chief of Police Timothy Rogan had his finger pressed down upon the black button. Kent was rather dreading the coming interview with his superior. All day long he had been thinking of the moment when, around eight o'clock in the evening, Rogan would be waiting for him in his office. Three days before, the chief had started away on his first real vacation in three years. Kent had thought long and hard before he sent off the telegram which told of the murder across the street. When he sent it, he knew Rogan would be back without delay.

The sound of the buzzer died away for a second only to come shrilling on again, a vicious ring, thought the inspector, threatening a long, stormy session. With a sigh he rose to his feet, and with a mass of reports under his arm slowly walked out of the room.

The hallway he went down was long and two feeble light bulbs failed to take away all the gloom. There were dark shadows in the corners, odd splotches of darkness playing over the doors he passed by. Not until he reached the end of the passage did he stop. With a little shake of his head he glanced at the closed door before him.

He was not only mentally tired but physically worn out. There had been no sleep the previous night, no chance to rest during the day, nor was there any rest in sight. It would be hours before he would be able to leave the station, and even when he did get to bed he doubted if he could sleep.

He hesitated a moment before the closed door, then pushed it open and entered the chief's office. The room was below the level of the street, with three long, narrow windows at the rear.

Seated in a large chair, behind the desk in the center of the room, was a short, stocky figure with snow-white hair. The hair was in wild disorder, as though the big hands holding the newspaper had been run through it again and again. Moreover Kent was far from being encouraged by the look upon the round red face.

Rogan's eyes were glancing at the headlines in the paper. It was not necessary for him to look very closely, for the heavy black letters could be read across the room, yet Rogan was looking at them with the incredulous gaze of one who did not believe what he saw, the look of a man shocked into startled wonder by what he read.

As Kent came across the floor, the paper was thrown upon the desk, and the chief coldly stared at his inspector. He said nothing however, waving a hand to a chair as he turned to reach into a drawer of his desk. When he found a stogie, his white teeth snapped off the end with a quick, angry motion, and the first gust of smoke was vigorous.

Kent knew his superior well enough to realize that it was no time for him to speak. There were those who said the chief was tough and hard, others who claimed he was without sympathy, but one thing was never said—that he was unfair or dishonest.

That he was efficient was admitted even by those who disliked him. Growl he might, but his men loved him.

Silence lasted for almost five minutes. Once Kent saw Rogan's eyes glance down at the paper upon the desk, observed the angry scowl which swept the smooth red face at the sight of the headlines; then, suddenly, the stogie was yanked from the tightly shut lips, as the thick-set body leaned forward in the chair.

"In the name of God, Kent," came the rough voice, "what does all this mean?" A wave of his hand accompanied the question and he did not wait for the inspector to reply. "I go away for my first vacation in years and your telegram wakes me up at three in the morning and tells me of a murder in the public library." There came a wondering shake of the white head, as a half scowl crossed his face.

"A murder in a public library. Never before in my life have I heard of one in that setting. And right across from the police station at that. When I get back here at seven, the papers are yapping that their police reporter almost got bumped off in the very same room. And then—then in my own office, waiting for me, was the police commissioner with the owner of the Star, just waiting to yell, wanted to know what the hell was the matter with the police."

Out of breath he paused, gave Kent a long, keen glance then shot out:

"Now what have you found?"

The inspector did not reply for a moment. What had he found? Twenty-four hours of activity had resulted in nothing. Clues there were none. Motive? Not even in his wildest thoughts could he think of one. Though his department had been busy, yet after all he had little to report to his superior. His eyes wandered over to the windows. From the street came the noise of passing cars, the shrill call of a newsboy. For a moment he glanced at the wheels passing above the windows, and the hurrying feet upon the sidewalk; then he turned and looked at Rogan.

The look he received in turn was shrewd, comprehending, with even a hint of sympathy. There was keen understanding in the dark-gray eyes which looked across the desk. The stogie had been thrust into a corner of the chief's mouth and stuck upward at a queer angle. For a moment the glance of the two men held and it was the chief who spoke first.

"You know, Kent," and there was a tone of weariness in the voice, "people just don't get murdered in public libraries. It's not done. This is the first thing of its kind I ever heard of. Of course as the library is a public place it will set the entire city talking. Tell me what you found."

It was a long story Kent had to tell; he knew Rogan would demand every detail. Starting with the call of the reporter, he swept on to the discovery of the body, the detailed police work, the fingerprinting of everyone in the library, the photographing of the room in which the crime had been committed. When he stopped for breath Rogan gave a grunt. There was surprise in the short expression, amazement upon his face. Bending across the desk his voice snapped out:

"You mean to tell me that woman was killed in her little office, while that big reading room filled with people?"

Kent simply nodded. There was nothing he could add.

"That seems impossible," was the quick retort "How many were in that room?"

"Fifty-three in the reference room, twenty-seven others in the building, and thirty-one of the library staff."

There came a short ugly oath from Rogan's lips.

"Hell, Kent, that means there were one hundred and eleven people in that building at the time of the murder. There were fifty-three sitting less than fifty feet from where she was killed. You say none of them heard or saw anything."

"Yes," was the admission. "No one in the reference room saw anything out of the way, and I'm afraid it's true."

There fell an uneasy silence. In it Rogan took; a pencil from his pocket, apparently to draw a serie of small circles upon the edge of the newspaper He was thinking, but his thoughts did not appear to be of great value. What could he think? A love affair in this case was absurd. The woman was over sixty.

Another thought swept over him. One hundred and eleven persons were in the library when the murder was committed. Fifty-three were almost in the very place of the murder. Not one heard or saw anything. No one could make him think that was true. What he was facing was a hundred and eleven suspects. A hell of a crime, was his conclusion.

Dipping into the desk, he found a fresh stogie and, as he lighted it, he glanced at Kent. The inspector was tired, with deep weary lines etching his face. Must have had rather an active twentyfour hours. Plenty of grief and no sleep. He needed rest and ought to be in bed.

"Kent," he questioned, "you have no suspects at all? Yet, on the face of it only one person could have committed the murder."

A startled expression passed over the inspector's face. Rogan's tone had been serious, yet at the same time there was irony in the tone. As Kent's astonished eyes met those of his superior, Rogan gave achuckle.

"Well, Kent, you told me no one was seen going into that little office. Then you have that reporter Rand walk into the place, and the next thing that happens was his calling the station. To make it look worse, you tell me the door leading into the passage-way was locked, so presumably the murderer had to walk through the reading room. Now the last person going into that office was Rand."

"You're crazy."

"Well, I don't think what I am saying is true. But what a case our District Attorney would build up out of those facts! Of course Rand knows nothing about the crime. Yet, under your story, there seems no one else who had the opportunity. And I remember a murder where the killing was done by a person who broke down a door to get into the room."

"How?"

"Well," said Rogan, "that happened a long time ago. It was in a rooming house in New York, about the time I started out in police work. A roomer on the top floor drugged his victim, locked the door, then told the landlady he heard a struggle in the room next to him. She went up with him, had him break down the door, and while she stood outside the door afraid to go in, he cut the throat of his man."

Kent shook his head. He had been startled by the chief's remark, but the twinkle in Rogan's eyes told him the chief was simply fooling.

"It's silly," Rogan went on, "to think Rand knew when he walked into that room what he was going to discover, and it's just as foolish to say he killed her; but, on your own story, no one else seems to have had the opportunity."

Kent nodded wearily, a gesture which had no meaning at all. The chief could do the talking; in his tired condition Kent would rather listen than speak. After all he had nothing of much importance to say.

"Now, Kent," was the question, "how did Rand happen to be over in the library last night?"

"I gave him the order which would let him into the building. He said he thought the clue to the murder must be in the building, so I let him go over."

"And he gets himself almost bumped off," was the dry comment.

"Yes. The lights suddenly went out in the reading room and Blake started to find out what the trouble was. He noticed the light was on in the little office, called out Rand's name, got no answer, so opened the door and found him on the floor, dead to the world."

"Humph," came the growl, "and no signs of who hit him?"

The inspector shook his head. They had searched the library again, discovering no one, nor was the weapon with which the assault had been committed found. Rand would recover from the assault, but it would be some hours before he could speak. It was Kent's idea that when he did he would be unable to tell anything of importance.

Rogan listened with his face expressionless. His eyes had darted over his inspector. Kent was a good man, slow, and careful, one that could be trusted to see that the usual police work was done, but it was creeping into Rogan's mind that the usual police work was not apt to get the department very far— not in this case.

To start with, the public library was an odd place in which to commit a murder, and the killing of a harmless woman, one over sixty years of age, did not appear to be explainable by any ordinary solution. "You have no idea what was behind Rand's being assaulted?" he repeated.

"No, chief," Kent replied. "It seems goofy. Nothing in that room was disturbed. There is nothing in it anyway but books. No money. The safe was locked. But at that Spicer told me there was nothing in the safe but a few old books. Why Rand got bumped and who did it we don't know."

Rogan gave vent to a short oath. Rising from his chair, he walked over to the windows, through which he glimpsed the lower part of the library. This held his attention for a while, then he turned.

"Got anyone over there tonight?"

"Two men. One on the first floor, the other on the second. They report to each other every ten minutes. But it seems silly. What can happen in that building?"

"Enough has," was the growling reply, as Rogan dropped down in his seat. "Plenty happened, and the city is going to raise hell with us."

He threw a quick glance at Kent. There were deep circles under the younger man's eyes and he was in sad need of a shave. The very manner in which he sprawled back in his chair spoke of a man weary to the point of exhaustion. What Kent needed was sleep, and that at once. A softer look crept into the chief's eyes and there was a gentle tone in his command: "Get out of that chair, George, and beat it home. Pound the pillow until eight tomorrow. Just leave those reports and beat it."

Insisting that there were still details to be gone through, Kent was cut short by the chief. Rising from his chair Rogan walked around the desk; his big hand dropped down on Kent's shoulder and he pulled him upright. Turning him in the direction of the door, he said but two words: "Get out," and followed them with a little shove.

When the door closed, he went back to his chair and, dropping down, stared moodily at the mass of papers upon the desk. There was a pile of papers almost a foot high, reports of all kinds which he must glance through before he could even know just what had happened.

As he lighted his stogie, he thought that after all he was getting to be an old man. Once a new crime would have aroused an eager spirit of excitement in his mind, but crime today was more or less a commonplace, sordid thing. He had seen so many sudden deaths in the past thirty-five years. Now here was another one to investigate. He realized that he was getting old.

Pulling his chair close to the desk he picked up the first report and started to read. For over an hour silence reigned in the office, broken only by the rustling of the papers or the drifting noises from the outside. When the last report had been read and placed back upon the desk, the chief made the first sound since Kent had left the room. The noise was a low suggestive whistle.

He had gone through the reports and it was even worse than he had feared. There had been plenty of information in the papers he had read, yet, now that it had been digested, it seemed of little importance. To try to reach any conclusion was useless.

The detectives' reports were of no value.

Leaning back in the chair, he reached out to pick up two sheets of paper upon which he had written a few notes. The sheets were not large, nor was there much written upon each page, just a heading and under it a few scrawled lines. Soberly he studied what he had written.

Place, was the first word. But nothing had been put down under it. That a murder should be committed in a public library was in itself an odd and startling thing for a police investigation. And to kill a librarian! At this thought the white head was slowly shaken.

Motive, came next. Under this heading he had drawn a large question mark. Nowhere in the reports was there the slightest hint of a motive. Yet for every murder there was always a reason, but he could not use the usual ones for this crime. They simply did not fit.

Searching through the crumpled mass of papers he found what he was looking for, the list of those who had been in the reading room when the body was discovered. It was a long list, covering over five sheets. For a while he studied, with a frowning face, the odd grouping of names. Among the fifty-three, he noticed two clergymen and three women well known in social circles. But there were other names upon which his eyes rested longer, names of men who had police records.

That they should be in the reading room did not surprise him. It had been a wet afternoon; they had gone there for shelter. Always public places draw the defeated, the semi-degenerate.

When he laid the papers aside, he had reached a conclusion. None of these persons would have the courage to commit a murder. If they did kill, it would be only under circumstances which offered absolute security. After all, they were mostly petty criminals, without much intelligence or any particular courage.

He had glanced at the report of the fingerprint expert, reading without a smile the vigorous note which was pinned to it. It was a note in which the expert reminded his chief that a public library was filled with fingerprints, you could find them anywhere you looked, and the expert had looked. But although he had fingerprinted all those who were in the library, the work had showed no results. There was one fact he would have to look into tomorrow. After Rand had been rushed to the hospital, the library had been looked over. Down in the basement a door had been found unlocked. No doubt the assailant had entered the building from this entrance.

There was a connection between the death of the librarian and the attack upon the reporter. Of this he felt certain, though there were no facts to bear out his conclusions. Whatever it might be called, hunch or intuition, Rogan felt that the two things were connected.

Rising he walked to the window and for a moment stood looking out into the night. Then he turned and started to pace his office. Back and forth he walked, pausing a second each time he reached the wall. He was worried, and he had an idea he would be worried a great deal more than he was now before the case was over.

The article in which the paper had told of the assault upon their reporter had been a vicious, ironic bit of writing. With sarcasm and bitter scorn the paper had attacked the police department. Rogan knew there was more than the crime itself behind the attack. For two years the Star had been trying to have him retired. Politics were behind the move. There were people who hated the chief because he could not be controlled. Until now the paper had been forced to keep in the background, but what a club they could use from now on.

The library was a public institution, everyone in the city entered it some time or another during a year. The murdered woman had been known to almost everyone. The paper was putting the hypocritical question: "Are public servants to be left unprotected?"

Trouble was ahead, Rogan knew that. He could picture the unjust criticism which his department would have to bear, criticism which might even break down the morale of his men. He had taken years to shape his department, a police department of which he was very proud.

His eye fell upon the telephone, and the sight of the black instrument caused a thought to flash over' him. Harley Manners had been out of the city all summer, but he must be home by now, and Rogan wanted to talk with Manners.

That the sixty-year-old police chief should be a friend of the wealthy and popular professor of abnormal psychology was a thing which caused many to wonder. But friends they were, the friendship going back to the days when, as a patrolman, Rogan stopped to talk to the little boy who played on his beat. More than once, out of his store of weird and odd knowledge, his psychological insights into the motives of people, Manners had proved of great help to the chief. Rogan had not forgotten the murder solved by Manners alone only the year before. He knew he needed help now, needed it badly. Looking at his watch he saw it was ten-thirty. A trifle late, but then, Manners never went to bed until the wee hours of the morning. He must talk to someone, someone who could bring a fresh insight into the queer crime. There was no one better than Manners.

With a determined shrug of his shoulders he made up his mind. Walking to the desk he reached down and dialed a number. Then he waited till there came a drawling voice over the wire.

CHAPTER EIGHT

With a long sigh of relief, Harley Manners threw the last letter upon the surface of the desk as his hand went fumbling into a pocket for his pipe. Slowly the long, expressive fingers patted the tobacco into a worn bowl, more slowly was the lighter used. Not until many smoke rings had floated away in a mist did he glance at the surface of the desk.

What he saw caused a disgusted scowl to sweep over the sensitive face. It was a long desk and the rosewood surface had been clear when he entered the house late in the afternoon. It was not clear now; instead it was a jumbled disorder of letters, magazines and book catalogues thrown everywhere. Just how many letters he had opened and glanced at only to throw the sheet back upon the desk, he did not care to think. Mail piles up if one goes away for a month, and during the four weeks refuses even to read a paper, mail which must be read when one returns home; and he had returned only three hours ago.

A hundred letters had been read, and he sighed thinking of the labor involved in the reading of them.

There had been a few bills, seven invitations from societies and clubs which insisted he must speak before them, the usual announcements of the organizations to which he belonged. The magazines had been simply thrown to one side, as for the book catalogues from every part of the world, these he had never even opened. Later he would spend a happy evening with them.

With a sigh he leaned far back in the big chair studying the room as though he had never seen it before. It was a room which was very dear to him, the place where he worked and dreamed a little, a room containing both the books and etchings which he loved. Yet, somehow, on this, the first evening he had been in it for a month, it seemed lonely and silent.

There were tall built-in bookcases on every side, where, behind glass, could be seen the books he had spent years in collecting. Black and white etchings mingled with gayly colored French prints; over the fireplace was the ship model he had bought in London. Flanking it, a long row of jade elephants marched to the end of the mantel.

The somber, studied glance which traveled down the long lengths of the bookcases would have surprised those who thought they understood the popular professor of abnormal psychology. For books were perhaps the great interest in Manners' life.

But tonight he was not so certain that he ever wished to look once more inside a book.

Years had gone into the making of that library. Every strange and curious social custom of humanity had its place on those shelves. Books upon the development of religious ideas stood close to the volumes which told of the Black Mass and the History of the Devil. Long rows of psychology were flanked by longer rows of history, and then of course there were the books on crime. Harley Manners had always been a disappointment to the social group to which he belonged. Why a young man who had all the money he needed should spend his time in teaching was a mystery discussed time and again. That one should work at all when it was possible to play was a problem far beyond the understanding of many who would have liked to call him friend.

At the University there were many professors who were more popular in faculty circles than Manners, but none so well liked among the students. There were scholars, who, when they mentioned his name, added that some day he would be the leading authority upon abnormal psychology in the country. But why this dreary subject should interest him his friends could not comprehend.

What they failed to realize was the great curiosity with which Manners had been born. Everything people did, and more especially the reasons for their actions, interested him. There was only one fear within his heart, and that was the fear that he might not know enough about everything.

This curiosity explained the many sections of his bookcases containing nothing but books upon crime. Every book dealing with the weird and curious bypaths of human behavior, all the accounts of famous crimes soon found a place upon his shelves. Crime had held his interest for years.

But tonight, as he glanced over his big living room, nothing about it gave him any pleasure. He had been away for a month and one might think that, after four weeks sailing the rough waters of Nova Scotia, the peace and the quiet of his room would appeal. There had been moments during the last month, when the little sloop had been outriding a gale, that he had longed for his library. Now he was in it and he was bored.

With eyes closed he sat half dozing in his chair. He was aroused by a growl from his dog. A log had fallen in the fireplace and the sound had roused the big Airedale, who had uttered a low, throaty remonstrance. Seeing his master move, the huge animal, twenty pounds larger than the usual dog of his breed, rose to cross the floor and thrust a cold nose in the man's hand.

For a while Manners let his fingers run through the wiry brown hair, then he rose to his feet. Crossing the floor, he pulled aside the drapery at the window and glanced out at the night. As he did so the dog, aping his gesture, thrust his nose against the window and gave a little whine.

The house was on top of a hill, and far below could be seen the lights of the city. He could trace the long outline of State Street, a narrow streak of flame, ending at the lighted tower of the municipal building. Lights were everywhere, street lights, house lights and the little creeping splotches of brightness from the headlights of moving cars.

For a while he stood glancing down at the city, then turning his head he looked in the other direction. The lake could not be seen, but the steady glare of the lighthouse upon the point was a glittering circle of yellow flame. Beyond it, far out on the water, seemingly motionless upon a great expanse of blackness, was the tiny starlike illumination of a boat at least twenty miles away.

He had purposely built his house for this view, and there never was a time, be it day or night, that it did not give him peace. By day the lake lay a shimmering mass of silver, stretched away to the horizon's rim. By night the city lights twinkled the activities of two hundred thousand people.

But as he looked out of his window, sensed the blackness of the night, there crept over him a feeling of loneliness. Not only was he bored, but there was a sudden need for companionship. Anyone with whom he could talk would be welcome, and, as he thought this, suddenly out in the hall a telephone broke into a long shrill ring.

Both Manners and the dog were startled by the sound, the animal expressing his opinion of the bell in his usual manner, a loud bark which rang through the room. Manners walked out into the hall wondering who could be calling. So far as he knew no one in the city knew that he was home.

The voice which came over the wire he knew, though it was a surprise to hear the rough tone. No one else had that heavy slow gruffness which was Rogan's. Before leaving the city Manners had been told all the details of the chief's coming vacation. Yet here was Rogan's voice coming over the wire. "So you are back," Manners said. In a momentary wait for Rogan's reply, Manners decided that the chief was worried. Not only was he worried but he must be greatly perplexed. When Rogan at last spoke, he said that if Manners did not mind he would run up and have a talk with him. Then Manners knew something had gone wrong.

Hanging up the receiver, he stood a moment glancing at the French phone. There was a perplexed line between his eyes, a little frown upon his face. Rogan had no business to be in the city, but he was.

There had been a worried doubt in the gruff voice, while the fact, that he would drive six miles at almost eleven o'clock at night showed that it was something important.

There was an odd friendship between the rough, uncultured police official and the intellectual professor. As a boy Manners had watched every day for the young policeman who came patrolling past his father's yard. Years later he had a good deal to do with the promotion which had come to the chief.

There had been many occasions when the chief dropped into the big library to present the problem he was facing. On two such evenings the advice given by the tall, quiet professor had been the thing which made it possible for Rogan later to announce that a crime had been solved.

Manners shook his head as he walked back into the room. Something was up; the chief rarely came around unless he was in trouble. What that trouble might be he did not know. For a month he had read no papers and what had happened in his city while he was away was outside his knowledge.

Sinking down in his big chair, he let his eyes fall upon the cluttered surface of the desk, and he rose again. Somewhere in the midst of the confusion was an evening paper. He had bought one as he drove into the city, but had tossed it upon the desk without giving it a glance.

Rummaging through the papers and letters, tossing aside magazines, shaking his head at the many book catalogues, he at last found what he was looking for. He sank down in his chair, lighted his pipe, then slowly unfolded the paper. One glance at the big headlines, and he sat upright, forgetting to keep the pipe going. When he allowed the paper to fall to the floor, its slow descent was marked by a shake of Manners' head. Not only had he read of the murder of Ruby Merton and the assault upon the police reporter, but he had read something else—a vicious, sarcastic attack upon the chief of police, the question why Rogan was out of the city, the hint that the time had come for a shake-up in the department.

Knowing his city paper, and having neither respect for its policies nor the way it was edited, the attack upon the police failed to move him. The paper was angry and would use the tragedy to strengthen its political alliances. But he sensed something the flaming headlines and the long news story did not say—that the police were confronted with a crime which was beyond them.

Murder in the public library of a large city, the victim a woman whom everyone knew. Manners knew his crime history, but try as he might he was unable to recall any previous case where a library was the scene of a murder. Murders and public libraries did not go together. Not one of the many books upon his shelves contained such a setting.

His glance traveled down to the paper upon the floor. It was the evening edition, the first story of the crime had come out in the morning issue. Some details no doubt had been omitted in the second telling of the story, but there were enough to make him wonder.

The woman had been killed in her own office, with over fifty people within sound of her voice. The police had no clues. That seemed incredible. How could a murder take place without the people in the reading room knowing something about it?

And to kill Ruby Merton! Though Manners never used the library much, having a complex about handling books which had passed through many hands, yet he had known the reference librarian. Why should anyone kill that harmless, neurotic old maid? True she had a sharp tongue, caused no doubt by the fact that most of the prizes of life had passed her by, but to murder her—the thought was absurd. Yet she had been murdered. That reality could not be escaped. For a few moments he allowed his wondering mind to work on the problem, only to give it up as a useless task. Until he knew all of the details there was no value in thinking. He would have those details when Rogan arrived. Now he knew the reason for the visit.

The thought caused him to rise from his chair and hurry out to his dining room. When he returned there was an odd shaped bottle under his arm and a glass in each pocket. Bottle and glasses found a resting place on the desk. As he placed them there he heard the sound of a car out on the driveway. Before Rogan reached the door it was flung open. As Manners glanced across the veranda he saw a taxi vanishing down the drive, then turned to watch the thick-set individual who was climbing the steps. The chief was moving slowly, as though he were either troubled or weary. Manners concluded he was both. He glanced into the kindly round face as their hands met, then led Rogan into the hallway.

Without a word the chief allowed his hat to be taken, and, not waiting for Manners to lead the way, walked into the living room. His glance took in the bottle and the glasses upon the desk, and, as he sank down in the chair, the paper lying upon the floor met his eye. Manners had seen the news story. Rogan was glad of that.

He watched his host open the bottle, saw the yellow liquid poured into the glass. As his hand clasped his drink he gave a little sigh. He was tired—weary physically, bothered mentally. As he took his first sip of the Scotch, his eyes traveled slowly over the room.

A shrewd, practical man was Rogan, versed in a world of hard, stern realities. Yet the long rows of books hidden behind the glass doors rather stirred his imagination. What they all might be about he did not know, nor would he ever find out. The fact that Manners no doubt knew everything which was in the hundreds of volumes had always impressed him.

Throwing back his head, he drained the glass, thankful that the smoky flavor showed the Scotch was old. There followed a long reflective look at the young man before him. The kind eyes rested upon the smooth face, observed the fine fitting suit, dropped down to glance at the dog, which had come over to lie at his master's feet. Then, with a shrug of his shoulders, Rogan waved his big hand at the paper.

"So you've read about the murder?"

Manners did not reply, though he did nod. The chief was tired, the faint scowl upon the red face was the scowl of a weary man, one not only anxious, but also perplexed. As he looked the chief's hand shot out for the bottle, and measured a very careful two inches into his glass. Then he spoke.

"They sure are giving the department hell, Harley, and it's nothing to what they will be saying tomorrow. I know that gang on the paper, they will use this crime as a club with which to hit the police."

Manners agreed; then for the next few moments they talked very much at cross purposes. Though Rogan expressed his opinion of the newspaper, Manners knew that it was not this which had brought him to the house. He was simply talking to hide his thoughts. Sooner or later he would reveal them. At last he started to talk about the murder.

It was a long story he unfolded, a story of absorbing interest to the psychologist. From the very first there was wonder in Rogan's voice. Murder did not shock him; that had been a commonplace event in his life. But that a murder should be committed in a public library seemed more than the chief could comprehend.

"Think of it, Harley. Did you ever hear of a fool crime like this, in a library, a place filled with books, with nice young girls and cranky old maids? What under heavens is there in a library to bring a crime?"

The grieved tone caused a smile to play over his listener's face, but he made no reply, and Rogan went on to give the details. From beginning to end the story was unfolded, and as the tale progressed there was one thing Manners could see very clearly.

The police had no idea as to the cause of the murder, no suspicion as to who might have committed it. Not until Rogan's voice died out did he speak. "A library as the setting for a murder is a rather unusual place—that is, a public library. But you are wrong about libraries being calm, restful places, simply filled with nice girls and nice old ladies. From the standpoint of a psychologist, anything might happen in some libraries I have known."

A stogie was being fished from Rogan's pocket, but at Manners' words his hand replaced the smoke and an amazed look swept his round face.

"Anything might happen in a library," was the startled comment. "What was that word you used? To a psyc—"

"Psychologist."

"What the devil do you mean by that?"

"Just this," was the reply. "You see, Rogan, the women in the libraries are nice women, as you say, and the building is very much a public place. They are dealing all the time with what we call the 'dear public,' and sometimes the public is not so nice. All day long they meet various types of people; some who are intelligent, and some—the majority—who are not. Nice people, as you say, but also neurotics, cranks, selfish people. It's not an easy task and often it does things to them."

"Does what?"

"I mean this. Many of the women in that building have been there for years. Their lives are cramped to the extent that they are a bit unnatural. As they grow older, like all people who have put away from them a home and children, they become a little selfcentered. Once, I suppose, there were more jealousies and more neurotics in our public libraries than in any other place, unless in the churches."

Rogan had listened at first with an amused twinkle in his eye, but it soon faded, and he glanced at his friend as though not just understanding what he was talking about. When the voice ceased, he took a stogie from his pocket, clipped the end, lighted it, then made a gesture with his hand.

"It's all very fine, Harley," he said, "but I don't see just what you are talking about."

"This, Rogan; once libraries were run only by women and by women who were given the jobs because of two things—family or position. They must earn a living and it was thought anyone could hand out books. So the libraries were filled with narrow, repressed, neurotic women, whose outlook on life had become a bit warped and soured. You see, in that case, instead of saying nothing could happen in a library, you should have said, anything might happen."

Rogan's face was a study of conflicting emotions. His brow was knit as if he was trying to decide whether he really knew anything about the public library which was across the street from his office. The look caused Manners to give a hurried explanation.

"In a sense that does not apply to our library. Spicer is one of the best men in his line in the country. The girls are all trained, girls who took up the work as a profession. It's a rather happy place, they tell me. Of course you cannot throw thirty some people together all the time without having some odd feelings develop, but—"

"Harley," broke in the chief, "I told you all the stuff Kent had picked up. Do you think that anyone in that building, anyone who worked there, could have killed that old dame?"

Manners had thought of that, but had dismissed the idea as improbable. He shook his head as he replied "No" to the chief's question. There fell a silence, broken by Rogan giving a sigh.

"You know, Harley," he said, "I don't like this sort of a crime. These odd crazy things are hard to solve, they do not fit into any picture you have. Give me the simple crimes, the ordinary killings."

"It's not the odd, the unusual, bizarre crimes which are the difficult ones to solve, Rogan. They are so unusual that as a rule their very oddity causes their solution. It's the commonplace killings, the ordinary shootings, which often are never cleared up. You know that, Rogan. The murders you have found the hardest to solve have been the plain, ordinary killings."

The chief nodded, Manners was right. Crimes which were out of the ordinary often were solved by the very fact they would not fit into any picture the police had. This crime was unusual. There was no doubt of that. He could not remember ever hearing of a murder committed in a public library. There should have been clues, lots of them, there were none at all.

Voicing his thoughts, he added that his fingerprint expert had reported so many fingerprints in the place that it seemed useless to take any. Prints were everywhere, on books, tables and desks. Hundreds could be collected if necessary, but they would not prove of any value.

"Nothing of value in that office?"

"No," was the reply. "There were fingerprints, lots of them, of every darned person who had been there for weeks, but nothing of value; at least that was what the report said."

Rogan gave a reflective glance at the bottle, then turned his head in the other direction. No more Scotch tonight. It was good stuff, smooth, smoky in flavor, but he would have to be going back to the office. Something might have turned up. But he had a question to ask Manners. After all, the professor knew more about libraries than he did.

"Harley, can you figure out any reason why that woman should be killed, would there be anything of value in the place?"

The question caused Manners to smile. In that library was all the beauty and intelligence which the mind of man has discovered during the entire history of civilization. Was there anything of value? Why the most glorious heritage of the world's life was. on the shelves of that building. In another sense the chief was right. Was there anything of value in that library? He doubted if there was.

Rogan was reminded that though the several hundred thousand books had cost a great deal, yet, in the strict sense of the word, they were of little value.

All could be replaced, and no one would commit a murder for any book the library possessed. As for money, there could be very little. Libraries never handled much money.

"Well," came the perplexed voice, "if there was no money and, as you say, no one in the place would kill her, that lets out the usual motives for murder. We must write off revenge, greed, and, in this case, there certainly could not be any sex motive. She was way over sixty. What's left?"

"Fear," was the retort, a remark which caused the chief to ask just what Manners meant.

"Fear often lies behind a crime," the psychologist replied, "fear of the consequences of exposure. Did she know some secret, so dangerous a secret that someone would risk murder rather than have it come out?"

"Humph," the chief growled. "Maybe fear did have some part in the thing. But who would be afraid of her?"

This was a problem Manners would have liked to have answered. He ran over in his mind what the chief had told him. Why had Miss Merton been so insistent in her demands to see Spicer? Whom had she tried to get on the telephone? Why had she been so excited? He put these questions into words, but received no reply. Rogan showing no disposition to speak, Manners went on:

"That might throw some light upon what happened. She had discovered something and that something excited her. She was, of course, a woman who was easily aroused, quickly excited. She tried to call someone on the telephone. Who and why?"

Rogan shook his head, saying he wished he had been in the city when the crime was discovered. There were loose ends to the affair, things not covered by the reports he had read. Among the threads to be unraveled was the matter of the telephone calls. He had an idea they would be hard to run down.

Silence fell between the two men. Manners lighted his pipe and through the smoke looked at the figure across from his chair. With his white hair sadly in need of a combing, sat a worried man, whose face bore a frown, between whose lips was an unlighted stogie. As Manners looked, the chief rose with a sigh and stood by the desk.

"Harley, this thing is going to be bad, with the paper riding us. I want you to come down to the inquest tomorrow. Just listen and see if you can get a hunch on anything. As a rule there would be no hearing, but the paper is yapping its head off, so we are going to please them. Too bad it was their man got the bump on the head."

He paused, looked at the Scotch, gave the bottle a scowl, then, making up his mind, reached down to pour a small drink. Holding it in his hand, he watched the liquid swirl with the motion of his wrist. He did not look at Manners as he spoke: "It's my idea that Rand's getting almost bumped off has something to do with the murder. But it's going to be hours before he talks. And at that I don't think he knows much. There was no evidence in the office when the cop found him. That gets me also."

Manners rose, poured out his first drink and, with the glass in his hand, stood looking at his friend. Rogan's last remark was no doubt true. The reporter had stumbled upon something that had to do with the murder, but until Rand was allowed, by the doctors, to talk, they would be in the dark as to what he had found.

Saying this, Manners insisted that he would drive the chief down to the city, a suggestion which was pleasing to the gruff official though he did make a half hearted refusal. Out of the house they went, the dog at their heels. It was the Airedale who climbed first into the big coupe, a gesture which did him little good as he was forced to get into the rumble seat.

The ride back to the city was a silent one. They turned out of the driveway to run down a steep hill. Far below could be seen the street lights, stars of flame against the blackness of the night. Like a flaming arrow, the main street divided the city into two sections, and the crawling lights of the cars glimmered like creeping lightning bugs.

At the bottom of the hill they started to run past the estates of the more wealthy citizens. Houses peered above high hedges; dark, tree-covered lawns were glimpsed, then, just as they reached the city limits, Manners turned to drive through the campus of the University, a campus dark and silent, with great buildings enclosing it on three sides.

Not until they reached the police station did Rogan speak, then it was to remind Manners of the inquest. With the promise that he would be there, the professor stopped the car, heard the chief say good night and watched him walk slowly into the station. With his foot on the gas he was just ready to start, when his eyes fell on the building across the street.

There had never been a time when anyone had said that the public library was a beautiful building. In the darkness it appeared a squatty, indistinct structure, which the lights from the street made a mass of vague shadows, a dark building, showing only one faint light; the last place in the world, he thought, where a murder would be committed.

With a start he realized that he was wasting time looking at the library, and started the car. Swinging into State Street he noticed that it was almost twelve. The street was deserted; only one building was a mass of lights. That was the office of the Star. As he saw it, he decided to stop.

There was but a block to go, and when he drew up to the curb to climb out, his first concern was to get the dog from the rumble seat and inside the car. As the reluctant animal climbed clumsily into the front seat, Manners grinned. Let anyone try to steal that car with Satin sitting behind the wheel.

He had been bored earlier in the evening, bored and lonesome. But as he pushed through the swinging doors of the entrance to the Star building, he felt very much alive. For a month he had done nothing but sail the coast of Canada, doing little thinking and no reading. Now there was a keen interest in his mind. Rogan had unfolded an odd tale. He might be able to help him in writing the ending.

CHAPTER NINE

The city editor of the Star was discovered in a long, narrow, cluttered-up office, tucked away just outside the reporters' room. The air was blue with the smoke from a corncob pipe, and the thin, red-headed gentleman pounding upon a noisy typewriter did not even raise his head at the intrusion. Not until Manners had spoken did he lift his eyes; then it was to stare at his visitor as though surprised to see him.

"Thought you were up in Canada."

Manners shook his head, reaching a hand down to the desk for the package of cigarettes which lay half hidden under a heap of copy. The red-headed editor was a close friend, and, though at times Manners wondered how Hart stood the neverending grind, yet he realized that if the editor were placed outside of a newspaper office life would seem barren.

"Got back today," was the admission, as, lighting the cigarette, he sank down in the chair by the desk to ask the brief question:

"Busy?"

The answer he received was short and terse. Hart sneered at the intelligence of a friend who at mid-night wandered into the office of the editor of a morning newspaper and asked such a stupid question. With the remark that he would be through in a moment, he started to pound the keys of the typewriter with his long fingers.

Leaning back in the chair, Manners watched the creeping carriage, then noticed three new drawings tacked on the wall since his last visit. There drifted to his ears the noise from the city room, the low rumble of conversation, the clattering sound of the typewriters.

Cutting through the discord was the sharp, metallic clamor of a ticker.

Ten minutes passed before Hart, with a jerk, pulled the paper from his machine, reaching with the other hand for a push button. His pipe was refilled, a match applied, then his chair creaked around as he looked at Manners. "He is after something," was the editor's thought. "Never knew him before to come into the office at midnight."

Seeing the glance, knowing what was behind it, caused a smile to pass over Manners' lips. Better get to the point at once. Hart was busy, but there was a brief pause in his work. Dropping his cigarette into an ash tray, Manners bent forward.

"Billy," he said, "I'm interested in that library murder."

"Well, who's not?" was the sharp retort, followed by a questioning glance. "Are you in on it?"

Manners admitted that Rogan had been to see him, an admission which caused a grin to sweep over the face of the city editor. The professor's next statement, that the crime puzzled him, caused a little explosion.

"That's a fine line. It puzzles us all. And that bunch over at headquarters are more mixed up than anyone else. They don't know why it was done or who did it, and it's been my idea some of those fool dicks think Rand himself did her in."

Rand's name gave the opening Manners was after.

"Billy, did Rand give you all the dope he picked up?"

"Harley," came the disgusted voice, "Rand picked up in that library the kind of story a young reporter always dreams will break. He discovered the corpse in a sensational murder. First we got was his telephoning in. He was told to stay on the spot until there was nothing more to pick up, then come back to the paper. I took him off his beat and let him have the story for his own to play with; it was his story. He wandered over to the station, after seeing me, then went back to the library. Somewhere around three in the morning the police were good enough to let us know he had almost been bumped off."

The last remark caused Hart to pause, and for a moment he expressed his opinion of the police. It had been five hours after the assault before his paper had been notified. To Manners, this partly explained the vicious attack upon the department.

"Why did he go back to the library?"

"God knows. Kent said Rand had an idea the explanation for the crime was in the building. So he was allowed to go over. You know Rogan likes him, and that's about all that we do know. Someone tried to bump him off. Why? Don't ask me. Until Rand is allowed to talk we don't know if he has any idea what happened. That's all we know."

Slowly Manners reached for his pipe, more slowly packed its brim with the strong English mixture he preferred. Rogan had been right, though the chief had expressed his opinion in the form of a question. The assault upon the reporter had something to do with the murder. The assault—his hand paused in applying the match—it was not an assault; someone had tried to kill Rand. Why?

As he lighted his pipe, he could see that Hart was very eager to return to his work, and knew that he must not delay him any longer. City editors had little time to spare when the paper was going to bed in an hour. But there was one more question to ask:

"All right, Billy, but was there anyone round here with whom Rand talked after the crime?"

The editor scowled as though trying to recall. He started to shake his head, hesitated, then spoke:

"When he left here to go to the police station I saw him talking to Wilson. But he's gone out to the Bagdad, trying to dig up a story there. I don't think Rand told him anything, don't think he had anything to tell."

Nodding, Manners rose to his feet, joked for a moment, said good night and left the room. Out on the street he stood beside the car trying to decide what to do. The wisest action would be to drive home and go to bed, but he did not feel like doing this. Three hours before he had been bored; now he felt keenly alive, very much awake. He would go to the roadhouse.

Starting the car, he went a block, then turned to go down toward the lake. Ten miles away, on a narrow, sandy point jutting out into the water, was the roadhouse. The proprietor was one of the many odd acquaintances whose names caused Manners' friends to shake their heads. Other speakeasies were raided once in a while, but Joe Zuko was like the morning sun; nothing ever bothered his place.

The streets, long vistas of dim light, were almost deserted; it did not take long to reach the outskirts of the city. By his side, the big head thrust far out of the open window was the dog, who once in a while whined in anticipation. The Airedale knew they were going to the lake; no doubt he thought he was to have a swim.

Once outside the city Manners let the car out. The road was a smooth white ribbon before the rushing headlights, which seemed to be piercing a black tunnel on each side of the machine. Trees lined the highway, trees he glimpsed as black lines as he sped past. Soon the road began to skirt the side of the lake and he caught the glimmer of a lighthouse far down the shore.

He turned off the road after a while to run over what seemed to be a narrow country lane, but the headlights showed that the dust had been oiled and bore evidence that many cars had passed that way. For a third of a mile he traveled, then stopped because the way was barred by a high wooden gate. Here he blew his horn three times.

He had to wait several moments before the gate was opened. Then a figure drifted out of the gloom and, under the glare of the headlights, he saw a short, stocky man lift a catch, slip through the gate and come to the side of his car. Before Manners could speak, a flashlight was played over his face. The scrutiny he received was brief.

As though satisfied by what the light had revealed, the man walked back to the gate and swung it open for Manners to drive through. Not a word had been said, or motion made. As he drove past the wire fence he saw the heavy, thick-set figure leaning languidly against the gate waiting for him to pass. The road he was now driving on was simply a rough path through the fields. Across a meadow high with grass it led, twisting and turning every few yards. Then came a stone wall, another gate, another field to be crossed, the second stone wall, and then he could see, far below, a building faintly revealed by two dim lights at widely separated windows.

The road sloped downward at a steep pitch, and as he neared the building the meadow gave way to a graveled parking space. Over this the wheels of the car crunched, then came to a stop before a high wooden fence. At least twenty cars were parked along the fence.

With a word to the dog to wait his return, Manners stepped from his machine. For a moment after his feet hit the ground he stood motionless. Before him was the long uneven outline of a one-story wooden building, from which no sound drifted and which, from where he was standing, showed no light.

For a moment he studied it; then started to walk to its farther side.

Turning the corner, he saw a light. As an illumination it was a feeble thing, simply a single lowpowered bulb, placed high above the outlines of a door. To his right the ground sloped down to the lake. Though the water could not be seen, there was a soft murmur against the shore.

At his touch the door opened, and as he passed down three steps he heard from far within the house the faint sound of a buzzer. The clatter lasted but a second, dying suddenly away. Before him was another door, with a closed slot at the level of his face. Overhead a brilliant light made the entry he was in as bright as day.

There came the sound of footsteps beyond the door and the sliding back of the shutter which closed the slot. A man's eyes were staring out at him, cold, impersonal eyes, searching every line of his face; then followed the sound of a bolt being withdrawn, the moving of a clasp, and the door swung silently open.

As he stepped into a hallway, he heard the door being closed and bolted behind him. He had been in the place before, had spent many hours listening to the life story of the proprietor. The doorman knew him. To the question whether Zuko was around, he nodded down the passage.

As Manners walked to the end of the hallway, he heard the sound of music from some part of the building. There was a small dance hall off the bar, and he knew that a three-piece orchestra was playing. But until he pushed open the door at the who had let him in. Opening the last door, he came out into a room which was at least thirty feet in length. Down one side, with a frosted mirror behind it, ran a mahogany bar, with three white-coated bartenders on duty. Seven men and two women were drinking, talking rather quietly as he entered. Across from the bar four tables were partly filled. He walked through this room, thinking, as he walked along, that though this was the best known speakeasy in the city, yet it was as orderly as a church. Noise and disorder were things Zuko never allowed in his place.

The room ended in a little hallway. The noise coming from the farther end told that there was a dance floor beyond. It was a short hallway, narrow and dingy. In the very center was a closed door. Here he knocked, opening the door when a gruff voice called out.

The room he entered had seen his presence many times, yet it always made his eyes open a little and caused wonder to creep into his mind. It was a large room, furnished with deep, expensive easy chairs, with a rare Persian rug upon the floor. Bookcases crowded with books, ran around three sides of the room. Upon the walls were a score of costly etchings.

He did not glance at these, looking instead at the short, fat figure seated in a chair by the big fireplace, a very short figure indeed, with round, drooping shoulders, a mountain of a man, oversized in weight and undersized in height. It had taken Manners a long time to make this room, with its etchings upon the walls and the overflowing bookcases, a suitable background for Joe Zuko.

As he came through the door the man in the chair turned to give him a look. The eyes which glanced across the floor were sharp and glittering. Steel gray in color, they hinted of a will which would brook no interference, of a power which might be overwhelming; but as they looked at the professor there crept into them a happy expression.

With a bound which was very rapid for so fat a man, Zuko was on his feet, advancing with outstretched hand to greet his guest. The smile which played over the fat face was one which held a hint of tenderness, if such a thing could be in Zuko's makeup. Though the palms which clasped Manners' hand seemed flabby, yet the grip was of steel, hinting of untold strength.

"Professor, I am much honored; it's been months since we talked here."

A wave of the hand swept over the books along the walls, as the low voice went on. "Now you sit here and I will get you a bottle of wine I have been keeping for you— Barsac, of the rare year, kept waiting for you."

The soft hands patted Manners' shoulders, pushing him down into a chair, stopping any words by a shake of the big head. Turning, Zuko waddled to the door, vanishing out into the corridor. His footsteps could be heard as they went down the hallway.

Sinking back into his chair, Manners took in the room. He knew what was in the bookcases—not fiction, not crime stories, but history, biography and, oddest of all, row after row of poetry. His glance rested on an etching, a Rops he would have given a good deal to own himself. Then his hand reached for the book Zuko had been reading, and the title, "The Early Romances of William Morris," caused him to shake his head.

Truth was stranger than fiction. Zuko was supposed to head one of the most notorious gangs in the country. At least, he had this reputation, though it had never been legally proved. His roadhouse had such strong political protection that, no matter what might happen to the others, he went along without trouble.

Yet here he was, in a book-lined room, whose walls were filled with rare etchings; and the owner of them all was the most notorious citizen of the state, a man whose name was synonymous with all vice and crime, yet a man who had one of the finest minds for literature Manners had ever known. Professor of psychology he might be; explain this streak in Zuko he could not.

An odd relationship had been established between the two men. Curiosity had caused Manners to seek the proprietor of the roadhouse. Something almost like friendship had been the result. Out of their conversations he had glimpsed vivid insights into human nature, which come to few men of his social class, pictures of almost another world, a cruel, hard-living world, of men at war with society, facing sudden death almost every hour. He had ended in liking the man, whom, no doubt, he should have despised.

The door swung open as Zuko came hurrying back into the room. Under his arm was a long bottle, in his hand two glasses. As he placed the wine upon the small desk, the round face broke into a smile. For a second his fingers caressed the bottle, then, deftly, he pulled the cork. Soberly he watched the golden wine fall into the glass. Then Zuko half laughed.

"Saved this for you, Professor. Don't often find this wine nowadays. Old, rare, aged, every drop a romance."

He paused, looking down at the bottle with a thoughtful air. There came a shake of the big head. "This bottle, Professor, came a long way. Bottled in France, then crossed the sea on a ship. Reshipped to the French islands, then on another ship. Some dark night a boat puts out from Long Island, creeps softly up to the ship; the bottle goes in the little boat. Then a wild dash for the shore, into a car, a fast ride into the big city. Then, some night, driving on and on in a car. Now you drink it. Adventure, romance all here."

There had been an eager sweep to Zuko's voice, and once, as he paused, his round face grew thoughtful, as though he were picturing the thousands of miles the bottle had traveled. When his voice died away, he gave a start; then he picked up the glass which he handed to his guest.

From his chair by the fireplace Zuko watched Manners take his first sip of the wine. He liked this man, admired his brain, enjoyed talking to him about the books he read, but at the same time he wondered what he was doing in his roadhouse. The professor had been out of the city for some time and as a rule never spent an evening with him unless he first called on the telephone and made the appointment. He wanted something; Zuko knew that. In a moment he knew what it was.

Placing the glass on the desk, Manners turned in his chair. The sharp gray eyes were upon him and, though the glance was warm and friendly, yet there was a question in the look. Taking a cigarette from his pocket, he lighted it before he spoke. Then, with a grin which made his face very youthful, he spoke:

"Joe, you know about this murder in the library?"

A surprised look flickered across the round face. Of course he had heard about the murder but he said nothing. Zuko never did say anything unless he was sure it was the time to say something.

"What I mean is this, Joe," Manners went on. "I know you hear a great many things that—that others do not hear. And, as you know, or read, the library was filled up with a pretty sorry crowd at the time the woman was killed. Did you hear any stories about the affair?"

The glance Manners received was a long, calculating one, but the response came at once: "You know, Professor, I do hear things." Not a muscle of his face moved as he spoke. "But this is a funny killing. No sense killing the old bird, none. No money, nothing to put her on the spot. Was a lot of bums in the library. Bums." He made a gesture of disgust. "None of them would have had the nerve to croak anyone. Not unless they could get them all alone. Do it quick when filled up with coke and cheap booze. Listen, Manners, no one in that room killed her."

"What makes you say that, Joe?"

The gangster was silent. A contemptuous look swept his face. Without speaking, he rose and crossed to the desk, refilled the glasses, handed Manners his own, then went back to the chair. Not until he had finished the drink did he turn to look at the professor.

"Just this, Professor. News creeps out in our circles. Somebody always talks; rumors get going. But not a thing of that kind have I heard about that murder. It was a rotten trick, killing an old woman in a library. You can be sure that none of the bums in there did it. If they had, I would tell you what I heard. I don't like that sort of thing."

From the contempt in Zuko's voice there was no doubt he had told the truth in his last remark. Contempt and disgust had been registered, disgust for the type of person who would kill, as he had put it, a harmless old woman. A thought however went flashing through Manners' brain. If all that was said was true, there had been other kinds of killings which did not make the man across from him disgusted. But he knew he had been told the truth; Zuko had heard nothing about the crime.

In the silence that came, he thought of this for a while. News did circulate in the criminal groups. How they knew all they did, he had often wondered. If any police character had been mixed up in the murder, Zuko would at least have heard the rumor. He had heard nothing and that fact was significant. He remembered after a while that he wanted to speak to Wilson and asked if he was in the place.

He received a nod, followed by the remark that the reporter was out on the dance floor. Though Zuko offered to get him, Manners rose to his feet, saying that he would look in the room himself.

Out in the hall he walked a few feet, then pushed open the door which ended the passage. The dance floor he stepped upon was small, for the tables along the wall took up a good deal of space. At the farther end was a raised platform, upon which a three-piece orchestra was pounding forth noisy jazz.

There were not many in the room, twenty at the most. Dropping down at the nearest table he sent his eyes searching for Wilson. The reporter had been one of his students at the University. In a moment he saw him. The expression upon the young man's face, when his eyes fell upon Manners, was a mixture of wonder and doubt, but at the invitation to come over to the table he nodded and, leaving the man with whom he was talking, crossed the floor.

That Wilson was wondering what he was doing in the Bagdad, Manners knew from the curious glance he received when the young man reached his side. But he dropped down into the chair and waited for the professor to speak.

There was not much that Manners expected to hear, though he had hoped that Wilson might have something to tell him. But when he had asked if Rand had mentioned any facts about the crime he had discovered, facts which had not been in the paper, or told to the police, Wilson shook his head.

Rand had said nothing.

He had met him rushing out of the city room to catch a quick meal before going over to the station. Rand had been very much excited, told him he had stumbled upon a big story, adding that Ruby Merton had been murdered at the library and, after saying this, Wilson remarked that that was the sum total of all that he had been told.

It was about as Manners had expected, and he had wasted a good deal of time in coming out to the roadhouse. For a second he wondered why he had followed the urge which had caused him to drive from the city after midnight, what subconscious drive had caused his action. More to say something than because of anything he wished to say, he laughed. "I wish I knew more about that library, Wil son," he said jokingly.

The orchestra broke into a sudden shrieking burst of piercing sound. Wild, barbaric wailing it seemed to Manners, filling the room with noise. Three couples hastened from their tables to swing into the dance. As they did so Wilson gave a little laugh. "Well, there is a girl out there who can tell you about the library," he commented.

His head motioned toward the couple who were dancing a few feet from their table. The embrace was close; the hips swayed suggestively, moving far more than their feet—a swaying couple, intimate, whose bodies were pressed close, whose every movement was sensual and revealing, a couple the same in height, with faces pressed close, cheek to cheek, expressing, in a public room, to noisy music, the world's primitive urge.

Manners knew he had seen the girl somewhere. Some might have called her good-looking, but not Harley Manners. The lips were too full, with a touch of thickness he did not like; the over-rouged face showed coarseness; the swaying body was large, slightly over-developed, with nothing one could call delicate in the lines. The large round eyes had a seeking, wandering look. As she danced, her body glued against her partner's, her eyes were searching the tables, passing over every man in the room. Only her hair was beautiful, titian hair, with a glow one did not often see.

As he watched, the woman's glance swept over to his table; for a second her eyes met his. There was bold invitation in the searching glance, a seeking question. Some, he thought, might think the woman beautiful, be attracted by the sheer physical appeal of her body, but not Manners. To him she seemed cheap, common, yet he was wondering at the reporter's remark. He put his wonder into a question.

"That's Stella Wellman," Wilson replied. "She has a job of some kind in the library."

Manners let his glance wander over the room, looked for a second at the tables flanking the walls, swept over three couples dancing upon the floor—rather common people he decided, dancing very suggestively—then turned back to the titian-haired woman and her partner. She did fit into the smokefilled room, but hardly into the staff of the library. He said as much.

Wilson gave a short laugh as he lighted a cigarette. Two puffs were taken, then he placed it on the edge of the table.

"Professor, some pull or other got her the job in the library. Spicer never has been very keen on her being there. She is supposed to represent the Chamber of Commerce and some of the other civic groups. She was put into the library to handle all the requests for information which come in to those clubs. They pay the bulk of her salary."

The swaying couple was passing them again, dancing very slowly, moving their bodies far more than their feet. The girl's face was flushed, the eyes half closed. After a searching look at the head pressed against the man's face, Manners decided that it was a very determined woman who was before him, one who would have her own way in life, though perhaps not always understanding why she wanted it.

"You would not think her husband would bring her here," he commented dryly.

Wilson had risen to his feet. At the remark he turned. An ironic smile passed over his youthful lips.

"It's not her husband. You see Stella steps out once in a while."

Manners sat at his table for a few moments after the reporter excused himself. Some vague, uneasy thought was trying to creep into a doubtful memory, but what it was he could not tell. He felt a little restless, as though puzzled by something he should remember. With a shrug of his shoulders, he at last rose to his feet and walked out into the hallway.

Zuko was in the same position as when he first came into the room. In the chair before the fireplace, a thin, little red book in his hand, the gangster sat reading. At Manners' coming through the door, the volume was thrown aside, as the huge man jumped to his feet. A wave of his hand motioned to a chair.

It was very late, and Manners realized that he should be getting home. It would be long after three before he could climb into bed. He was very weary. Explaining that it was far too late to remain any longer, he stopped the protests Zuko made. Some other time he would come early in the evening and they could talk till dawn.

The mountain of a man waddled out of the room with him, down the narrow passage and into the bar. There were still men whose feet were on the rail, talking over tall, half-filled glasses before them. At one of the tables two individuals were playing a game of checkers, making their moves without a word. Refusing an invitation for a last drink, Manners said good night and passed into the entry and out into the night. From the car came a sharp, insistent bark, as the animal, sensing his presence, stirred into life.

He drove slowly. The road stretched before him and not until he reached the outskirts of the city did he pass a car. A slight breeze had sprung up and a feeling of freshness was in the air, a hush upon the land. By his side the dog had slumped down upon the seat and, with his head resting against his master's knee, was sleeping.

He was thinking as he climbed the long hill which led to his house, still thinking when, after the car had been placed in the garage, he entered his living room. As the lights flashed on, he noticed that he had forgotten to put away the bottle upon the desk, and, picking it up, went to the kitchen. Filling the dog's dish with water, he soberly watched the animal drink and poured a finger of Scotch into a glass of water for himself.

The dog followed him to the bedroom, sinking down upon the rug with a deep sigh. Undressing, Manners turned the water on in the tub, and a few moments later, clothed in a gay pair of pajamas, he gratefully rolled himself into his bedclothes.

The bed seemed very soft and he was weary. For a while he lay motionless, thinking over what he had heard in the last few hours. It was an odd crime, but he felt sure that when the truth came out it would prove to be a stupid crime. One without any intelligence or sense behind it. But he realized that it might be a long time before it was solved, if it ever was.

His thoughts played for a while around the library. Then another thought came into his mind. He saw again the smoke-filled dance floor of Zuko's roadhouse. It was true that most of the people who went to the place had some standing in the city life, but after all they were cheap people, out for a passing thrill. What was that girl from the library doing there? After a while he gave up thinking and drifted off to sleep.

CHAPTER TEN

Sunlight came creeping through the glass windows of the breakfast room, dancing across the wide sweeping lawn, lingering upon the fall roses which climbed the side of the rambling stone house. Far down over the fields lay the lake, blue as the sky above the smooth, motionless water. Below the hill stretched the city, with the high office buildings etched in sharp, distinct outlines against the sky. From a tall factory chimney a blue ribbon of pale smoke trembled a hesitating line of shadowy vapor in the clear air.

It was his first morning at home in many days, and, after coming into the breakfast room, Manners had gone at once to the window and looked out at the view he loved. This morning, however, the glance he threw out of his window was very brief. Breakfast was on the table, but his first action after sitting down in his chair was to pick up the paper lying by his plate. One glance at the heavy headlines and he decided that he would eat before reading.

Breakfast over, he lighted his pipe, then went over to the window and took the easiest chair in the room. There was a good deal to look through, for the Star had devoted five columns to the crime.

When the paper had been thrown to the floor, he realized that the information behind the five columns of small type was, after all, very meager. The bulk of the long article was a bitter attack upon the police, an attack filled with scathing sarcasm directed against the police commissioner. There was trouble ahead for Rogan; Manners could see that, with, perhaps, a shakeup coming to the police force. Leaning back in his chair, he thought of the unjustness of the news story. The paper was demanding that the police department get into action. How could they expect Rogan and his men to get results when the crime seemed to be one without any clues? If there was such a thing as a crime in which the murderer left no clues behind, the murder of Ruby Merton filled the bill.

This fact intrigued Manners. Writers of mystery stories were always talking about the perfect crime.

From his long study of criminal records, he knew that there never had been a perfect crime, any more than there had been a super-criminal. The criminal of high intelligence did not exist. Men of intelligence were not criminals. There were clues in every crime, there must be in this one.

He was forced to admit, from what Rogan had told him and the account he had read in the paper, that clues appeared to be absent; nor did there seem to be any reason for the crime. It was true abnormal persons, persons who were emotionally unbalanced, did at times commit murder without any apparent reason. Was this a crime of that type?

It might be. He knew the reference librarian, realized that she worked for a small salary, had no close friends nor any real enemies. To find a motive for her death would be a difficult task.

For over an hour he thought over all that he knew of the murdered woman. She came from one of the old families of the city. In her childhood they had been wealthy, but the influence and money had vanished years ago. She had been a soured, neurotic old maid, whose tongue poured out irony and contempt. But this alone was not enough to cause anyone to kill her.

He smiled at a thought. If all the women in the world who were neurotic, whose tongues were spiced with hatred and intolerance, should be murdered, the police would indeed be busy. But no, the cause of her death could not lie in her unfortunate disposition. People did not like her, but that was as far as the feeling would go. They might despise her; they would not kill her.

A glance at his watch told him that it was time to drive to the city for the inquest. Some unknown motive lay behind the crime. Not only was there a reason, but he felt certain that the murder was not the sudden impulse of a moment. There was calm, deliberate planning behind this crime, a motive which must have seemed overpowering in the mind of the murderer.

The thought was with him as he drove down the long hill and into the city. It seemed impossible that anyone should kill the reference librarian in her own office, with over half a hundred people a few feet away, but Manners was positive of one thing: The crime, and the place where it had been committed had been skillfully planned.

He stopped in front of the courthouse, seeing at once that it would be impossible to park. The curb was lined with cars as far as his eyes could see; there was no break in the parked machines. People were pushing their way up the stone steps, all sorts and conditions of people, an eager, morbid crowd, anxious to get into the building.

The attendant of a near-by garage received the car, and Manners hastened back to the courthouse. To reach the door was a difficult task, but at last he managed to make the attendant look at his police card. With a shrug of his shoulders, the man opened the door, allowing the psychologist to enter.

The corridor was jammed with excited men and women. At its farther end he saw the steps leading to the second floor. To reach the courtroom he Would have to press through that closely packed crowd and in some manner get up that stairway.

From where he was the task looked impossible.

Then he recalled that only a few feet away was the door leading to the police commissioner's office. If he could reach it, a back stairway would take him to the:second floor.

There was only fifteen feet to go, but it required fifteen minutes to push through the crowd. Fighting his way forward, struggling past closely packed bodies, he managed to slide along the wall till his hand fell on the door knob. To his relief the door was unlocked, and in a second he had slipped into the small office.

There was a patrolman seated behind the cluttered desk. He started to rise indignantly as the door opened. A glance, however, caused the man to nod and point to another door at the other side of the room. Without a word Manners hurried into a back hallway. Here a short flight of stairs led upward.

The courtroom occupied almost all of the second floor of the building. To Manners' knowledge, it had never been used for an inquest. He understood why it was being used now. The bitter newspaper campaign against the police had caused the officials to give the widest publicity to the hearing. From the crowd in front of the building, the closely packed people in the hallway, he realized that the largest auditorium of the city would not have been able to take care of all those who wished to attend the hearing.

To his embarrassment, the door he came through brought him directly into the courtroom. The judges' bench was before him and below it the lawyers' tables; he was facing the jury's box. To his first glance it seemed impossible that there should be room for one more, for the place was crowded. Every bench was filled, people were standing two deep along the sides of the room, lining the wall by the door.

Walking past the bench he noticed Rogan talking to the District Attorney, and, seeing Manners, the chief pointed his finger at a chair close to the witness stand. As Manners dropped down into his seat, he saw the coroner's jury had already been chosen; he gave a start as he noticed the men who were sitting a little to the right.

It was not the ordinary coroner's jury. In the first seat sat the city's best known clergyman, his round face set in a stern expression. The four merchants seated below the clergyman were the leading merchants of the city; a banker flanked a well-known doctor. Manners smiled when he saw the mild face of the professor of English; it was the face of one who seemed to be wondering what he was doing in such a situation.

Behind the judge's bench sat the coroner, a doctor who for many years had been more of a politician than a physician. As he glanced at the coroner, Manners decided that the man was not only nervous, he was worried. Evidently the situation was far from his liking; the look upon his face was that of a man who wished he were somewhere else than in the crowded courtroom.

The lawyers' tables had every seat occupied. This was to be no ordinary coroner's hearing. Manners had been to many hearings marked by little interest, rushed through as rapidly as possible. This inquest would not be rushed through. Public feeling, fanned into flame by the paper, had caused the police to bring forth their strongest batteries.

Close to a long table, Rogan was talking to the tall, thin District Attorney. The chief had put on a new uniform, whose buttons shone like gold, and it was very evident that he was worried. His round face was a deeper red than usual, and, as he listened to what the attorney was saying, he kept shaking his white head.

Whatever the argument was about could not be told. It was apparent that the chief did not agree with what the District Attorney was saying. After a vigorous shake of his head, Rogan turned to beckon Kent to come to his side. As the head of the Homicide Bureau rose from the chair he was sitting in, Manners turned to study the room.

An undercurrent of excitement was playing along the crowded benches. The low hum of eager whispers hung over the room; feet were being shuffled nervously upon the floor. It was an eager, curious crowd of men and women, brought forth partly by morbid curiosity and because a well-known woman of the city had met a violent death.

The sudden, sharp pounding of a gavel upon the desk reverberated through the room. The hum of conversation died away as people stirred and looked toward the coroner. The inquest was about to start, and the physician had risen to his feet to stand behind the desk.

There was only a brief statement of the crime.

The spectators were warned they must remain silent; at any disturbance the room would be cleared. From the picture the coroner drew of the crime, Manners decided that the man knew very little of what had taken place. He wondered if anyone knew.

It was soon evident that the inquest had been staged more to satisfy the newspaper than for any other purpose. Because the public had been aroused, the police were doing what seemed to be the wisest thing, taking the public into their confidence. Manners soon realized that the time would be wasted. Inspector Kent, the head of the Homicide Department, was the first witness called. The audience watched the tall man climb into the witness box and waited eagerly for his story, but when it was told they were scarcely any wiser than before.

He described the telephone call which had come from the library, telling of Rand's excited voice as he told him Ruby Merton had been murdered. He went into details in picturing what he saw as he entered the room. A shiver of excitement passed over the crowd when he described the cord that had been around the woman's neck, mentioned that the body was still warm. There was nothing he could tell beyond that.

The police doctor who followed him was also brief. In his opinion the death had taken place not more than twenty minutes before he saw her. The body was still warm, and he was very positive that she had not been dead long. Strangulation was the cause of death, the cord having been drawn very tightly around her throat.

In rapid succession three men followed each other upon the witness stand. The first man was a well-known clergyman who testified that he had been in the reading room all afternoon. To his knowledge, no one had entered the "little office, except two girls and a man. He had seen the librarian come out of her office some time after she had received the last visitor.

The two other witnesses only added to the minister's story. They also had seen three persons go into the office and had noticed the woman walk out into the reference room long after her last visitor had departed. They admitted that they had not paid much attention to the walled-off office. Perhaps someone might have entered when they were not observing it. But the very manner in which they said this told that they did not believe anyone had done so.

There would be no results, Manners thought. The police knew nothing. The inquest had been staged more to let the people of the city see just how difficult was the task of solving the crime than for any other reason. The expression upon Rogan's face made it plain that the chief had discovered no new information. So far the hearing had proven a dreary affair.

A quick glance over the room showed that the spectators had the same thought. When the first witness had gone upon the stand a nervous undertone of. excitement had swept over the room. Men and women had leaned forward; faces filled with anticipation; eyes were bright, but at this moment their faces bore a rather bewildered expression. They had expected excitement; there had been none.

"Mary Hunt," called the District Attorney. From somewhere behind the rail which ran across the front of the room, a tall, well-dressed young woman rose to go up to the witness box. As she seated herself, Manners remembered that he had seen her around the library. The answer to the first question told him that she was one of the two girls who had gone into the little office the afternoon of the crime.

Her testimony, however, was brief. The reference librarian had wished a book from the stacks, and she had taken it to the office. As for the door leading out into the hallway, she was unable to say whether or not it had been locked, but she thought it must have been, for they all knew that Miss Merton never allowed it to be otherwise.

When she stepped down, another librarian took her place. This girl was dark, with a keen intelligent face, well poised, sure of herself. Her testimony was given in a low soft voice and her answers were very brief, because she had nothing to tell. It had been close to four o'clock when she went into the office, but she had tried the hallway door and she said that the door was bolted and the woman's voice had come from within the little office.

"What did she say?"

"Come through the reference room and enter in the usual manner."

"Then Miss Merton knew it was you who tried the door?"

The girl nodded.

There came a pause as the District Attorney gave a half despairing look at the police commissioner, then suddenly bent down to whisper to the head of the Homicide Bureau. What the two men were talking about was not easy to tell. It was the inspector who was doing the bulk of the talking, bending close as though to give some information to the attorney.

In the pause Manners again turned and studied the crowded room. He knew many of the people there, women from up on the hill, college professors, doctors, and even clergymen—the sort of people who, as a rule, never attend a police inquest.

Then, just as he was about to turn his head away, he noticed a man looking in his direction. This man was seated just behind the rail which divided the room, a thin man, with a little black mustache, dressed, Manners decided, just a little too carefully, but the eyes which passed over him were bright and, to his surprise, filled with an eager interest.

As Manners turned his gaze away, he tried to recall who the man might be. Where had he seen him? For he knew he had seen him somewhere.

Then all at once it came to him. Why that was Henry Harlen. No doubt he was at the inquest because they were going to use him as a witness. Even as Manners thought this, the man's name was called. As the thin, well-dressed man seated himself, it was clear, from the look he cast around the courtroom, that he was a man very sure of himself, one who never doubted that he was among the world's elect. The glance which swept the courtroom was a proud glance, a curious glance, one in which distaste was mingled with contempt.

Manners had met Harlen, but the two had never been more than acquaintances. Once, the man had been professor of history in a western college, a position which he claimed to have resigned, which others claimed he lost. Having some money, he came to the city, where he spent the greater part of his time in the writing of sarcastic essays for the more liberal magazines. When the man started to give his testimony, Manners had just decided that he knew very little about him.

His evidence was given in a low voice, but one having an odd, sharp, disagreeable edge to its inflection. He had come to the library early in the afternoon to see Miss Merton regarding some research he wished done. He added that she had done some work for him in the past, for which she had been well paid. As for the door leading into the hallway, he knew nothing about it. In fact he was in the office only a short time, perhaps fifteen minutes. Then, for some unexplained reason, he volunteered the information that the librarian had appeared a little excited, a bit nervous. At this remark the attorney sprang into action.

Did he know what made the woman nervous, had she given any hint as to the cause of her excitement? These questions caused a half smile to pass over the thin lips as there followed a shake of the head. There was a bored note in the voice which said that he had not the slightest idea in the world as to what made her nervous and excited. He only knew she appeared that way to him.

He was dismissed after this, leaving the stand with the air of a man who had performed a disagreeable duty. Why he had been called, Manners could not understand. Long after Harlen's visit to the office, the last visitor had tried the door and found it locked. Harlen's testimony seemed a useless waste of time.

The District Attorney was looking over the room, his eyes searching over every settee, glancing down the long lines of men and women. He was looking for someone. When he turned to glance down at Rogan it was clear that he had failed to discover the person for whom he was in search. Walking to the judge's bench, he held a short conversation with the coroner, then went back to the table.

The coroner's eyes searched the room.

"Is Mr. Spicer in the room?"

There was no response, and after a moment the request was repeated. Everyone knew who was wanted. It seemed queer, thought Manners, that the well-liked librarian was not at the inquest. Apparently he was not, for though the coroner called his name three times there was no response.

The non-appearance of the librarian appeared to have caused some confusion. Rogan, Kent and the District Attorney were in a conference. Their chairs were pulled close, their heads bent together. A rather heated conversation it appeared to be, in which Manners saw Rogan shaking his head, saw the inspector rise to his feet and carefully study the room.

Odd that Spicer was not present. He had made the city library one of the five most efficient in America. He loved every book upon its shelves, every thought which played around it. Yet at the most sensational event the library had ever known, the inquest over the death of Ruby Merton, Spicer was absent. The man must be ill, Manners thought, an idea he dismissed at once. If Spicer was ill the chief would have been notified. Something must be back of it. Then he heard a name called.

"Stella Wellman."

He saw the woman rise and come to the gate leading through the rail. As she passed by him, her dress brushed his chair and there came to him the overpowering odor of a deep perfume, a perfume which he knew was far from costly yet was very strong. As she sank down into the chair, he studied her with interest. There was too much rouge on her crimson cheeks, the lipstick had been over-applied. Even her dress was a bit garish, for the sash wound around her waist matched the glory of her titian hair. But as she crossed her knees to lean back in the chair, he knew most of the men in the room would find her attractive.

A few hours ago he had seen her swaying figure moving suggestively over the dance floor in Zuko's roadhouse. Now she was a well-poised woman, though there was a hint of caution in the glance she threw down toward the chief. The overdeveloped body hinted of strength, and the swing of her shoulders, as she settled back into her chair, bespoke determination and selfwill.

But, like the other witnesses, she knew nothing of any value. She did say that there were several who held keys to the private office of the librarian. She herself had not been in the reference room that afternoon. As for Mr. Spicer, he had been in his own office from two o'clock up to the moment when he was notified that the woman was dead.

When she stepped down, Manners wondered how much longer the inquest could continue. Evidence there was none, no hint of motive, no knowledge beyond the mere fact that a crime had been committed.

He realized that if the papers had not been attacking the police department no inquest would have been held. Under the state law an inquest was left to the discretion of the police commissioner. This one had been held to show the public how unfairly the paper was acting. He doubted if the police had any evidence against anyone.

A moment later he knew that they had none. The attorney rose and told the coroner they were through, apologized a little to the jury, telling them that, though they had wished to show the manner of the crime, yet at present they did not know why it was committed, or by whom. They had no other evidence to introduce.

A murmur of astonishment swept the room.

There came the sound of shuffling feet, people broke into excited whispers. Manners did not blame them for being surprised. Of all the inquests he had attended, this was the oddest, remarkable for the failure to produce evidence, the absolute lack of knowledge shown by the police about the crime.

The foreman of the jury beckoned to the coroner; that official left his desk to walk over and speak to the city's best known clergyman. There followed a brief conversation, and as the coroner walked away the foreman turned and spoke in a low voice to his jury. Whatever it was he said could not be heard, but a nod went down the line of twelve men.

The verdict followed a moment later, a verdict given without the jury leaving their seats. It was the usual one, of murder and by unknown hands. There was no other verdict they could give. As the coroner announced that the hearing was over, the people rose to their feet. Manners hoped the unsatisfactory hearing would have the effect the police desired.

As Manners rose from his seat, Rogan caught his eye, following it with a motion of his hand. He was pointing below, suggesting that Manners go down below to the chief's office. Nodding in reply, Manners started through the courtroom. It was a slow passage, for the narrow aisles were jammed, and he found the crowd at the door very difficult to get through. In the end he managed to reach the hall and get down to the first floor. A moment later he had knocked at the chief's door. Receiving no response, he pushed it open and entered the room. No one was in the dingy office, so he sank down in a chair and lighted a cigarette. He glanced toward a window through which he could see hurrying feet out on the sidewalk. Curious, Rogan had always stuck to this dingy room; for some unknown reason the chief had a warm feeling in his heart for the place. It had often been suggested that he move to another floor, but always he had refused.

The door was violently pulled open and, from the way it was slammed shut, he knew Rogan was in a temper. The footsteps which pounded across the floor were not those of a happy individual; the manner in which the heavy figure dropped down into the chair showed that the chief was very much disgusted. The sight of the flushed, scowling face glaring at him across the desk caused Manners to laugh.

"Chief," he ventured, "do you know that in every murder case there are ten clues?"

The look he received made him chuckle. As if wondering whether he had lost his senses, Rogan scowled at him for a moment, then, digging a stogie from his pocket, placed it between his teeth and snapped off the end with a vicious snap.

"And who was the damned fool who said that?"

"Scotland Yard," was the grinning reply. "In the little book of instructions given every new policeman, they claim that in every murder there are ten clues, always. Those are the clues the murderer leaves behind him."

"They do, do they?" came the rough growl, as with a jerk the stogie was pulled from the chief's lips. "Ten clues in every crime. I wish to hell they could see this murder. Ten clues. Why there is not even one."

He paused and looked at the fingers on his right hand as though he had never seen them before. Bending across the desk he started to check off the outstretched fingers.

"Ten clues in every crime. Answer these five questions for me, Harley, and I can get somewhere. First, why was she killed? Second, how in the devil did anyone get into that office and not be seen? Third, who hit Rand on the head? Fourth, why did they do it? Fifth, did he get a glimpse of the person who did it?"

He paused, as another thought came sweeping across his mind. Picking up the stogie he replaced it between his lips. His voice grew confidential.

"Harley, it struck me damned funny Spicer was not down here for that inquest. You know you can say all you want about clues; you have to have them. But I'm getting worried. Got a hunch."

There was no superstition in Manners' makeup.

To the professor of psychology, what Rogan called a hunch was something which could be explained. The subconscious was beginning to stir, giving a , vague warning that something might happen. It was warning, based upon past forgotten knowledge, and upon some recent fact. He knew that Rogan had often said that a good police chief must know when to play his hunches.

"Yes, got a hunch, Harley. I don't think this thing is over. Don't know why I feel that way, but I do. Think something is going to happen. Feel it."

The rough voice died away as suddenly Rogan turned in his chair and looked upward at the windows. When, after a long look, he whirled in his chair, there was a grave undercurrent in his voice.

"Something else is going to happen, Manners," he said gravely. "We have every detective in the city running around in circles. They are looking for things. God alone knows what they are looking for. I don't. Trying to find some secret in that old maid's life, dig up stuff about the library staff. They have found nothing, nothing at all.

Even failed to find anything about the cord around her neck, except that over forty stores sell it. But—"

The rough voice died away. A sudden silence crept for a moment into the low dingy room. It was broken by the shrill honking of a car out in the street. As the sound died away, Rogan spoke again.

His words were slow, the tone thoughtful, with an undercurrent of nervousness which Manners could feel:

"You mark my words, Harley, it's not over. Something else is going to break. And I wish to God I knew what it was and where it will happen."

CHAPTER ELEVEN

Through the weaving smoke of his cigarette, Manners gazed thoughtfully across the desk. He observed the snow-white hair, noticed the expression which passed over the smooth-shaven face. Though a professor of abnormal psychology, who perhaps should laugh at all references to what Rogan called "hunches," yet he did not feel like laughing. Instead he was beginning to reflect the chief's uneasiness. Many had been the discussions between the two men as to the value of scientific technique in the solution of crime and the part played by intuition. Again and again had Rogan testified that a good police chief must know when to play his hunches. Scientific technique was all right; they needed all they could secure; but there were times when it failed. There was something, claimed the chief, an instinct to feel one's way through a case, the warning that evidence was not what it seemed. Intimations came at times which defied all reason, but which Rogan insisted often led to the solution of crime.

The theory might appear unreasonable, but Manners knew that it was based upon a psychological truth. Some little forgotten incident had stirred the vast storehouse of the sub-conscious, whispering that something should be remembered, warning that, under similar circumstances in the past, certain things had taken place. Such was the procedure now taking place in Rogan's mind. The chief was uneasy, afraid of the past, very much worried about the future.

Manners might have put these thoughts into words if the door had not opened to allow Kent to come into the office. The tall inspector was carrying a number of reports in his hand. As he stopped before the desk, a quick glance took in the two men as with a disgusted tone in his voice he spoke:

"Rand has just told what happened to him."

Rogan stiffened to attention as he snapped out a question:

"What does he know?"

"Not a damned thing. Said he was kneeling by the safe, heard a sound back of him, started to turn, then bang, and he was out."

With an expression of disgust, the chief violently threw his stogie on the floor and rose to his feet and stamped on it. With both hands gripping the side of the desk, he leaned over the cluttered surface to glare at his inspector. The shake of the head he received caused him to sink back in his chair.

"No," was Kent's comment, "there is nothing he can tell us. The doctors won't let us ask him any more questions till tomorrow, but he told us all he knew."

"Kent," growled Rogan, "you let him go over to the library that night. Have any idea what he was going for?"

"No. We were talking. Rand said it was his idea the reason for the murder must be in the library. He had nothing to back up the statement. Asked me to give him an order to Blake. Blake was on duty there. What Rand expected to find I can't see. We had gone over the place with a fine tooth comb."

Manner's eyes narrowed as he listened. So far no reason for the killing of Ruby Merton had been discovered. The reporter might have been correct.

Somewhere in the library, better still, in that office, might be the cause of her death. There had to be a cause. Find it, then one could begin to have a theory. A theory. How many times had he heard someone describe a crime as being like a stone thrown into the middle of the pond. The vibrations went swirling out in ever increasing circles, which in the end reached the shore. If it were possible to start with the very outer circle, one would be led to the heart of the pond, to the very center of the disturbance. So with a murder. Perhaps the most obscure fact was the one which would lead to the solution. Kent broke in upon his thoughts:

"Chief, no one mentioned anything about a book salesman who came to the woman's office around two o'clock."

Rogan shook his head as if the incident was of little value. But the book salesman was a new individual to Manners. So he asked who the man might be. The information that he was the first of the three persons who went into the office during the afternoon caused a retort:

"Then there were four instead of three."

"Four what?" growled out Rogan.

"Four individuals who entered her room. Two girls testified that they went, then there was Harlen. The book salesman makes four."

A disgusted expression swept over the chief's face. He threw a questioning glance at his inspector, and received a prompt reply:

"That's right, chief. But you see there is nothing about that to get excited over. Spicer told me a publishers' salesman came into the place around two; he sent him in to see Miss Merton. He was only there five minutes. Three others were in the office later. We were told there were but three, but the girl in the outer room overlooked one of the two women who went in."

The mention of the librarian's name stirred afresh an uneasy feeling in Rogan's mind. Spicer should have been at the inquest. It was not like him to neglect his duties. The library was the pride of his heart. That, after the greatest tragedy in its history, the man whom it most concerned had failed to be present at the hearing, was something he could not understand.

He shook his head, glancing at his watch. Time for lunch. It would be a busy afternoon. When he returned to the office he must get the librarian on the telephone. Where was it he lived? Oh, yes, he had it. The Waveland

Club. Better have the man on the telephone switch put in the call at once. Have him tell Spicer he wanted to see him.

Manners refused the invitation to lunch. He was not hungry and he had developed a desire which he now put into words. Turning to the chief, he asked if the office where the murder had been committed was locked, receiving the reply it was and that Kent had the key.

"Let me give it a look."

He was informed that it would do him more good to have his lunch, but if he wished to examine the office he could. There was a little sarcasm in Rogan's voice as he insinuated that it was time someone with intelligence searched the scene of the crime. But the tone told Manners he was being reminded that the place had been carefully looked over.

When he walked into the large lobby of the library, he was surprised to find it more or less empty. The girls behind the delivery desk were idle, and as he entered the reference room he noticed but three people sitting at the tables. Over the place hung an uneasy silence, and the quick nervous glance he received from the two women behind the lending desk showed that they were nervous.

He paused for a second before the glass door of the built-in office, then, inserting the key, stepped in. In order to be free from interruption, he locked the door behind him, and stood motionless, taking in the room. A bandbox of an office, simply a walled-in space where one could be alone. His glance took in the bookcases along the wall, rested for a moment upon the safe, passed over to the desk in the center of the floor. There were two chairs, one near the safe, the other on the opposite side of the desk. He saw the chairs and his eyes narrowed.

He could picture what had happened. The woman had been sitting in front of the safe, the murderer had walked behind her, no doubt first clasping a hand over her lips so that she could not cry aloud. Then he strangled her. There was no doubt in his mind that the murderer must have been someone she knew. No stranger could have gotten behind her, taken her off her guard.

He thought of this for a while, then, certain the theory was correct, walked to the nearest chair and sat down. Someone she knew. He remembered what Rogan had said. All morning she had been trying to get a number on the telephone. Spicer had said that she had tried again and again to see him early in the afternoon.

Nervous and excited. Well, in a sense she was always emotionally upset. The library staff were accustomed to her vagaries. If they had thought the day of the murder that she was excited, then her actions must have been unusual. If so, something had come into the routine of her life, throwing it out of its usual balance.

Turning, his glance swept the room, resting upon the door which led out into the hallway. What was it Rogan had said about that door? Oh, yes. They had found it unlocked. After the crime the murderer had turned the key and escaped through the hallway.

There was the greater problem as to how the person had gotten into the room.

The last one who had entered that room had tried the door and found it locked. When the girl left, the woman had come out into the reference room. No one had seen any other person enter her sanctum. But someone had, someone who had committed the crime.

His eyes narrowed as he studied the door. There had been a key in the lock. Even though the individual had another key he would have been unable to open the door. It was easy enough to understand that the murderer had left by that door. All he had to do was to turn the key, then step into the hall. But how did he get into the room?

A thought swept over him. All day long the neurotic old woman had been greatly aroused. Again and again she had tried to call someone on the telephone. Three or four times during the afternoon she had made an effort to see Spicer. Something had excited her, shaken her out of the usual routine of her life. Perhaps here lay the explanation of how anyone had entered the room.

Suppose she had managed to get her party, say, during her noon hour. The individual had been asked to come to her office, told, because she wished to see him secretly, to use the door leading from the hallway. If that were true, she herself turned the key to allow the individual to enter. That must be the explanation. There was no other.

A hand went reaching for a cigarette, but as his fingers closed upon the case he remembered where he was. With a little smile he withdrew the hand. He was satisfied with his last theory. Ruby Merton herself had opened the door, what was more, had invited the person to call upon her. What had happened after that?

He thought he knew. Murder was committed for three reasons. They were the background of most crime. There were murders which had a sexual background, jealousy, betrayal of faith, murders in which one only had to find the woman and the motive became clear. This could not apply here. No one could think the sixty-year-old woman had been killed for that reason.

There were murders committed for gain. Money, however would hardly enter into this crime. She had a small salary; there would be no money in the office—he checked himself on this, remembering the story of the money found upon the desk. But the forgotten fact only made his reasoning the more correct. It had not been stolen, though it was in plain sight of the murderer. And of course, a library never had anything of value upon its shelves.

He came to the third cause of murder. To him, fear was the outstanding motive in crime. The murderer had been afraid. Afraid of being exposed, afraid of the law, afraid of a hundred things. Push that fear to the breaking point, and certain types of individuals would kill, in a sudden raging frenzy.

Was this back of Ruby Merton's death? What had that old woman known, what secret had she stumbled upon? If he knew, then they would at least have something to start with. She had been nervous and excited all day. No doubt she had managed to get her party on the telephone, had insisted that he come to the office. It would be someone she knew, and in a sudden rage he had killed her to stop her tongue from speaking.

What could she have known so important that someone would rather kill her than take the chance of her speaking? That it should concern the library seemed absurd. Yet she had wished to see Spicer and after his return to the city had made three attempts during the afternoon to see him. If she had reached him, she would have told the secret within her mind.

He studied the safe for a moment. As a rule libraries do not have a safe, have little need of one. The steel cabinet was not very large, though it had an air of security. Rising, he crossed the floor and tried the dial, giving the door a jerk as he did so.

The effort was wasted; it refused to open. He studied it for a moment, then turned to walk out of the office, to go over to the desk of the reference room. It was a silly request he was going to make; he doubted if the woman in charge of the room could gratify his wish. He was a little surprised when she told him that she did know the combination of the safe. After he had shown his police card she jotted down four numbers upon a bit of paper.

Back in the office he closed the door and went over to kneel before the safe. His fingers had started to twirl the dial of the second number when a sound caused him to turn. It was a slight scraping noise, the sound of a key being inserted in a lock. As he gave a quick glance at the hallway door he saw the handle slowly turning.

The key was in the lock on the inside, so he knew that the door could not be opened from the outside. For a second he looked, then leaped to his feet. So sudden was the jump that his foot went under the leg of the chair and it fell with a crash to the floor. At the sound he heard the key being pulled from the lock.

With a bound he was at the door, his hand fumbling with the key. As it turned, he gave a twist of his wrist, flinging the door open. Two steps and he was in the hall in time to see the door leading to the lobby swing back, but he recognized the figure hurrying away. That bright sash he had seen around the waist of Stella Wellman when she sat in the courtroom.

His first thought was to hasten after the girl, make her tell why she had tried to enter the office. His second was more intelligent. She would simply make some excuse, and it would not be true. If there had been any real reason for her visit, she would not have hurried away when she heard the chair fall. With a little frown between his eyes, he closed the door. After locking it, he went back to the safe. In a moment the door yielded to his pull, swinging open. Why he was interested in the safe he could not tell. Perhaps it was because it was the only thing in the room which was locked. But when he gave the first glance into the shadowy interior he shook his head.

There were compartments which he discovered were closed. Below the two compartments ran a series of small shelves containing nothing but reports, books, and what appeared to be five book slips. There seemed nothing of value in the safe. Habit more than anything else caused him to pull out the books and look them over. There were a few first editions, a Keats, four Conrads and an edition of Science and Health. They were fairly valuable; someday they would be worth a lot of money. Replacing these, he went down to the next shelf.

This shelf amused him. Spicer was an educated, cultured librarian, so there were no censored shelves in his library. But the few books which Manners glanced at had been thought just a little too frank to be on public display, books dealing with sex, with several studies of the social customs of the ancient world.

For a few moments he looked at the titles, most of which were in his own library. "Das Erotische Element in der Karikatur" was flanked by the "Secret Museum of Naples." An eighteenth-century edition, no doubt the first, of a rare French poem, "Parapilla," held his attention for a while. He wondered how it had come into the library's possession.

When this was laid aside he picked up a thin volume, smiling as he read, "Le Libertine de Qualite."

The other books were of little value, evidently having been placed in the safe because, after all, they could not be placed in general circulation. A work on sex whose pictures were more lurid than the text, was the last thing to be replaced upon the shelf.

Then he went down to the last shelf. There were five book slips to be looked at, and he pulled out their contents before glancing at any of the pamphlets. The first one he picked up caused an envious wish to pass over him. He gave a rapid glance at the other four, and there was a little jealousy in his mind as he read the titles. He would have liked to own them all.

He picked up the first pamphlet to reverently turn the pages. Seventy-two small pages they were, but he knew he held in his hand the rarest and most valuable of all American books, the famous Mounts Relation. It was the first printed account of the Pilgrim fathers, written by John Bradford himself. What was more, the thing was worth four thousand dollars, and someday would be worth five times that sum.

With a sigh he placed the pamphlet aside, to pick up the next. This was smaller than the one he had just looked at, having only two-thirds as many pages, but it was almost as rare. A smile crossed his lips as he thought that the "Discourse on Civil Government" by John Davenport had been printed in Cambridge in the year 1663. It was worth about two thousand dollars.

Placing it aside, he gave just a glance at the other Mounts Relation, sighing as he thought of the luck, of a library in owning two copies. The two remaining pamphlets were looked over, but he discovered that they were of little value. Then, with his hand resting upon the earliest printed book in America, he let his thoughts run wild.

Books were more than a hobby with Harley Manners. He loved them with a devotion and reverence which made him thrill to anything in print. He was thinking, wondering if the day would ever come when he would discover two rare items like the ones upon the floor—just a few faded sheets of paper, aged by the years, covered with dim yellow letters, yet worth thousands of dollars. At this thought he gave a violent start and his hand shot down to pick up the Mounts Relation.

"Faded paper and letters yellow with age." But the pages he was turning were not old, nor were the letters yellow with age. Instead the paper was white, the printing jet black, with letters sharply new before his amazed eyes. As he took in these things, he did two things. First a long low whistle escaped from his lips, then he reached down for the other two pamphlets.

As he laid them aside there was a startled expression upon his face, a look of wonder in his eyes. His eyes kept going down to the floor as though he refused to believe what he had seen. Three pamphlets had been looked at. They should have been faded with the years, the printed letters paled by the passage of time. But these pamphlets were not old, nor were they worth very much money. In fact he could have bought the three of them for fifteen dollars. Instead of three rare, historical booklets— pamphlets worth over ten thousand dollars, the slip covers contained only reprints. Because of its great rarity and the fact that libraries were unable to secure the originals, because of their great worth, the Mounts Relation had been reprinted several times. The same thing had been done with the Davenport booklet, the last reprint having been put out only two years ago. They were exact copies of the originals, but there was this difference: Where the original pamphlets were worth thousands of dollars, the reprints were worth only three or four.

For a while he sat on the floor, then putting the three pamphlets in his pocket, he placed the other two in the safe and closed the door. As he rose to his feet he stood for a second looking at the green steel safe. His face was very grave. He knew now why Ruby Merton had been excited, knew why she had been murdered.

The shelf inside that safe should have held three pamphlets, worth around eleven thousand dollars, but the rare editions were not there. They had been replaced by cheap reprints whose value was not over eleven dollars. The two rare firsts of the Mounts Relation, the original edition of Davenport had been stolen; the reprints had been substituted.

He knew now what the librarian had discovered when she came into the library. He could well understand that she would be excited, nervous and worried. He knew why she had tried so frantically to see Spicer, what she wished to tell him. What was more, he had discovered something else. He knew why she had been murdered.

CHAPTER TWELVE

With his back pressed against the desk, Manners stared vaguely over the tiny room. For a moment his mind was far away, recapturing a memory. He could see the dark, tumbling waters which only a few days ago he had sailed upon, could picture the frowning coast of Newfoundland, bleak and desolate against a low black sky. He remembered one evening when a wave of loneliness had swept over him.

The same feeling was with him now. In his pocket he could feel the pamphlets, just a few sheets of white paper, pages covered with black letters. He knew, though why could not be explained, that they had been the cause of the woman's death. They had been wanting a motive for the woman's death; they had one now.

He was uneasy. There were very few persons who remembered that the library possessed the early Americana. Nine years had passed since they were willed to the library; in that time the gift had been forgotten. As for that, the general public would know nothing about the pamphlets, have little knowledge of their rare worth. Only a book collector would be interested.

He shook his head. Rack his mind as he might, he could think of no one who would steal them. He knew the three book collectors of the city; none of them collected early Americana. Someone who knew that the pamphlets could be easily sold might have stolen them. Yet there was a flaw here.

The pamphlets had been taken from the slip covers and reprints substituted. Whoever had done this knew months might pass before the substitution was discovered. It must have been an individual familiar with the library, someone who knew that the pamphlets had been reprinted. This led to but one conclusion.

Could it be anyone on the library staff? As a rule librarians were not bookish people, so one could bar out almost three-fourths of the staff. The average assistant would know little about the pamphlets. Spicer would. As Manners thought this, he realized that there was another shock coming to the popular librarian. The murder was horrible enough; the loss of the rare items in the safe would be the last straw.

Suddenly he thought of the girl who had tried to enter the office while he was kneeling before the safe. She had known that the office was locked. The police had insisted that it remain closed until they gave the word for reopening it. She had a key. Why should she be interested in the room? If her interest was a legitimate one, why had she hastened away upon the discovery that someone was within?

With a shrug of his shoulders he turned to open the door. It was no time for theories. They would have to wait. Rogan would be back from lunch; the news he would tell him would cause the gray eyes to open wide in surprise. As he hurried from the building he smiled as he thought of the coming interview.

It might be difficult to make the chief believe that any book was worth four thousand dollars. Rogan's life was one in which books played no part.

The chief was behind his desk, apparently busy with a mass of reports. The air was blue from the smoke of a strong pipe, the white ruffled hair looked as though it had never felt a comb. Rogan was busy and Manners could tell that he was not over pleased with the interruption. Lighting a cigarette the visitor pulled a chair close to the desk.

"Rogan," he said suddenly, "I have an idea I have found the motive for the murder."

The report fell upon the desk. The white head shot back as the cold gray eyes studied the professor's face.

The look was one of doubt, filled with a startled wonder. For a moment the eyes of the two men held; then Manners slowly nodded his head.

Assured by the gesture, Rogan's lips opened:

"The hell you have."

Manners swept into his story. Because he knew the chief had no knowledge of the value of rare books he went into careful details. Vividly he pictured taking the books from their slip covers. Carefully he described what he had found within the covers, telling what should have been there; then he spoke of the rareness and value of the pamphlets. Silence fell upon the room when his voice died away. Rogan slowly shook his head, then, drawing a knife from his pocket, very deliberately cleaned the bowl of his pipe. This done, he carefully packed the burnt bowl with tobacco, lighted the match and applied it. As the cloud of smoke rose to the ceiling, his hand went across the desk.

"Let's see those things," he demanded.

Taking the three pamphlets from his pocket, Manners placed them in the outstretched fingers.

The glance Rogan dropped down to his hand was a curious mixture of doubt and wonder. For many moments the big fingers turned the thin pages; not until each item had been looked through did he raise his eyes. Then, placing the pamphlets on the desk, he gave a doubtful shake of his head.

"Are you sure, Harley, those few pieces of paper are worth all you said!"

"Not those," was the retort. "What should have been in those slip covers was worth around ten or eleven thousand dollars. The Mounts pamphlet sold a year ago for thirty-five hundred. The library owned two of them. The Davenport item was worth twenty-five hundred. It's my idea the three things would bring eleven thousand now."

Rogan gave a doubtful shake of his head as he glanced at the desk. Eleven thousand dollars for a few old pages of paper. Why a man could buy a house for that.

What any person in his right senses would want of those old books was more than he could see. But Manners knew about such things; if he said they were worth that, then they were. But there was one thing he wished explained.

The thin booklets he had been told were reprints. What did Manners mean by that? He was informed that the originals were so rare that book collectors and libraries were unable to secure them. Several times copies had been printed, faithful copies, even down to the quaint lettering and odd spelling. The reprints, however, were of little value.

"So it's your idea, Harley, that someone stole the original books and put those three things in their place?"

Manners nodded, seeing Rogan's face grow gray as he gave a doubtful look at the desk. He knew it was difficult for his friend to realize what had taken place. That any book should be worth much money was something Rogan would doubt. He saw the perplexed shake of the white head.

"Ten thousand dollars for three old books. That's a lot of money. But there is one flaw in what you say. What was to stop the library from having sold them long ago?"

"They could not sell them. It's nine years since Rice died—and his will contained a clause that they must not be sold until ten years passed by. They have been stolen all right."

"And you think the old lady found that out on the morning she was killed. That was the reason she was all excited and went rushing round."

Of this Manners felt certain. The early Americana were the most valuable items the library possessed. They were kept in the safe, no doubt were scarcely ever looked at. At long intervals they might be brought out and shown. Ruby Merton must have discovered on the morning of her death that they were gone. What was more, she had an idea who had taken them.

There seemed no doubt of this, and he went into a long explanation to prove his point. The librarian was a secretive soul, jealous of her position. No one would have been taken into her confidence except Spicer. He, however, had been out of town and did not return until noon. During the afternoon the woman had tried three times to see him. Manners was positive she wished to tell him the pamphlets had been stolen.

Rogan listened attentively, nodding his head in agreement. They now had a motive for the murder.

Yet it was the most absurd motive he had ever stumbled upon. Because three books had been stolen, a woman had been killed. He voiced a question:

"So you think she knew who took the things?"

"Yes. That is why she was trying all morning to get someone on her telephone. She knew who took them. The murderer killed her in order to prevent the exposure which would come when she talked. No doubt she threatened him."

A doubtful look swept the face of the chief.

"We have no idea when they were stolen. It may have been weeks ago, may have been only the day before the crime. But when you say she threatened the murderer, you are saying he did more than kill her. He must have talked with her before committing the crime."

Manners agreed with this. He told Rogan the pamphlets would never be allowed to leave the library. No one could borrow them. In order to be seen they would have to be looked over in the office.

The substitution must have taken place under the eyes of the librarian. What was more, she would not allow everyone to see them. Not only was she cranky at times, but there had been moments when she seemed to think the library belonged to her instead of to the public.

"But, Harley," was the protest, "you forget something. If some outside person substituted those pamphlets, they had to be clever. You forget the people who work in the library. Some of them have a key to that office. They knew about the things in the safe; more than one person would have the combination. It would be easy for someone in the building to have taken them. How about Spicer?"

Manners laughed at the mention of the librarian's name. He reminded Rogan that Spicer had been in his own office at the time the woman was killed, asked him to remember that the woman had been trying all afternoon to see him. Sarcastically he inquired if Rogan was trying to accuse the man of stealing his own books.

The irony was a wasted effort. Very soberly Manners was reminded that Spicer might be able to tell them something they did not know. Then Rogan's face grew anxious. He expressed roughly his desire that the librarian would come into the office, added that he wished he knew where the man was. There was something in the tone of his last remark which caused Manners to throw him a quick glance.

"Did you call the club?"

"I called the club. He went out last night about ten and has not been back since. I left word for him to call me, but have heard nothing from him. It seems funny to me that—"

Whatever it was he thought, Manners did not discover. The anxious voice died away as Rogan turned in his chair to stare moodily out of the window. Only for a moment did he look, then the chair was whirled around.

"What do you say, Harley, was it an inside or an outside job?"

Starting to shake his head, Manners stopped. Again he heard the scraping sound of the key being inserted in the door leading from the hall. His eyes saw once more the vanishing form of the Wellman woman. It was an odd incident, something Rogan should know about. He told of the episode, adding that he had seen her the night before at the Bagdad.

When he had finished there came only two words:

"Describe her."

The description finished, the chief's hand reached for a button and he gave it a vicious bang. The white teeth snapped shut.

"Flashy, common, gold-digging type. If she works in the library she ought not to be dancing at Zuko's. We will have that little lady looked up."

Manners might have retorted to that remark, but the opening of the door stopped the words he intended to say. Kent was hurrying across the floor, a Kent who looked far less weary than he had in the morning. He paused at the chief's desk listening to the barking command which came:

"Kent, over in the library is a girl named Wellman. Flashy dame, not the type to be there. Look her up, get all the dope you can on her. Do it at once."

With a nod of understanding the inspector turned toward the door. One step was taken before the chief's voice caused him to turn. His eyes followed Rogan's pointing finger, a finger directed towards the desk. There was doubt on Kent's face as he picked up the pamphlets, a doubting question in his eyes when, after a brief glance, he replaced them on the desk. What they were, or why Rogan should be interested in them, he did not know. Yet the chief was interested.

In a few short sentences he was informed of what Manners had discovered. At the mention of the value of the stolen items, the inspector cast a doubtful look at the desk. The sincerity in the chief's voice told him that his ears had not deceived him. The three little books were of great value. Rogan's voice ended in a command.

"Keep your eyes open, Kent, but for a while say nothing about these things having been stolen. I want to see Spicer first, then we can get busy."

Kent nodded, his grave look still fixed upon the yellow slip covers. With a nod of his head he started for the hall. One hand was on the door knob when he paused and turned around. His voice expressed the question in his mind:

"Then you think, chief, the motive for that old dame's death lies right on your desk? If that's so, then you get what was back of the attack upon Rand."

He paused to give his superior a chance to speak.

There came no words, only a sharp look from the cold gray eyes of his chief. Seeing that Rogan intended to remain silent, he continued:

"You say they were in the safe. I suppose the person who hit Rand thought he was just about to open the thing. If he did, there was a chance the substitution would be discovered. That was why the person tried to kill him. If that's so, then whoever took the pamphlets, the individual who murdered the woman, is the same person who hit Rand. What do you think?"

There was no reply for a moment. Rogan cast a thoughtful glance at the pipe which lay upon the desk, changed his mind and reached into a pocket for a stogie. After it was lighted he took four long puffs, then whirled around in his chair.

"Guess you are right. That would make Harley's theory as to what's back of the crime correct."

"Fear," Manners commented. "I have an idea fear is back of this, fear of being exposed. The murderer committed his crime because the stealing of the pamphlets had been discovered. When he saw Rand by the safe, having committed one murder, he was willing to kill again to prevent the motive of his first crime being known. Again, fear."

"But, Professor," broke in the inspector, "I don't see how bumping off Rand would have prevented the library from finding that those things had been stolen."

"It might have been weeks, even months, before the library discovered that a substitution had been made. They were not things often looked at; the yellow covers in which they were kept would have stood upon the shelf until someone familiar with the items examined them. That might have been the next day, the next week. On the other hand, months might have passed before the substitution was discovered. No, the person who tried to get rid of Rand knew what he was doing."

Kent started to make a reply, but a wave of Rogan's hand towards the door caused him to walk out into the hallway. As the door slammed shut, Manners glanced at his wrist watch. It was two forty-five. Time he ate. Breakfast had been a long time ago; he was beginning to feel hungry. On the verge of rising, he sank back in his chair as the door opened. A patrolman was coming across the floor, carrying mail in his hand. Without a word, he deposited the letters upon the desk and left the room. As the door closed, Manners half rose, saying he would leave. Asking him to wait a moment, Rogan cut the first envelope and pulled forth a piece of paper.

Leaning back in his chair Manners lighted a cigarette. He was tired, with a weariness which contained some exhilaration. The visit to the library office had brought an unexpected result. He knew that it was only luck that he had been the one to pull the pamphlets from their slip covers. The police might have looked at them, but they would never have known what had happened.

The thought caused him to throw a glance at Rogan. Leaning far back in his chair, the chief was reading a letter. As Manners glanced he saw Rogan throw it into a basket and reach down for the last envelope. He watched the heavy fingers jerk at the end of the envelope, noticed the sheet of paper pulled forth.

The white head bent over the paper, then a sudden start jerked the heavy body into a stiff, upright position. A startled exclamation escaped from the chief's lips as his eyes glued themselves upon what he was reading. The astonished expression which passed over the round face was one which caused Manners to lean forward in his chair. It was an odd expression—doubt, mingling with wonder, which in turn gave place to a sudden horror. For a moment the red face flushed to a deeper crimson; then the color slowly faded from his cheeks. The eyes glancing at the letter were the eyes of a man who did not believe what he saw, and the hand holding the paper trembled. Something was wrong, what?

Slowly the chief was rising to his feet. It was not a deliberate movement, more like the unconscious act of a man pulled upright by some force within him. For a second he stood by the desk, a hand resting upon it for support. Then he looked at his friend, and the look was an appealing cry for aid. He slowly extended his hand. In it lay the white sheet of paper.

It was a single sheet of heavy, costly writing paper which Manners took from Rogan's hand. There was no date and the typewriter which had written the black letters must have had a new ribbon. At the end of the letter was a scrawling signature which he did not glance at. He started to read, read only three lines, then gave a little cry of amazed, protesting horror at what he saw.

If you will go to the Hunt estate and drive past the sunken garden, you will find my car. In it will be my body. It would only be a question of time before you would discover that I took the pamphlets and sold them. Miss Merton found out what I had done. I had to kill her to escape exposure. But I know there is no chance of final escape, so am taking the easiest way out. Henry Spicer.

He read the short message twice before he could believe what it said. Spicer had committed suicide, confessing that he was guilty of theft and had committed murder. The letter told the police where they could find the body. He raised his eyes and looked at Rogan.

The chief was standing beside the desk, and the look upon his face was that of a man not exactly certain of what had taken place. As the eyes of the two men met there came a sudden gesture from the police chief; slowly his arms went out in a half circle and just what that gesture might express Manners could not say. Then came the voice, slow, questioning, hesitating.

"So I was right, Harley. Something was to happen. Something did. Spicer—" He paused as if even he doubted what he was to say.

"Spicer all the time. Kills himself, committed the murder. It's all over."

Manners' glance went down to the sheet of paper. It was still in his hands, a white sheet covered with heavy black letters, which confessed a crime, told that a man's life had ended. Rogan had said that all was over; he was not so certain. A surging doubt was rising in his mind. Lifting his head, he met Rogan's eyes and something in his glance caused' a question to frame on the chief's lips, a question he did not have to put into words, for Manners was speaking, in a grave, hesitating tone:

"Over, Rogan? No. It's just started. We'll find that Spicer was murdered, discover that this letter is a forgery."

CHAPTER THIRTEEN

Rogan's hand had been creeping nervously across the cluttered surface of the desk. His fingers were searching for the button which would call the emergency department. As Manners' voice died away the chief's fingers went shut, and he threw a hurried, incredulous glance at his friend. Had his ears deceived him? Could it be that Manners doubted that Spicer had committed suicide? One look into the eyes boring into his own, then:

"Harley, what are you trying to tell me? What—"

The words faded as his eyes fell upon the envelope Manners still held in his hand. It was an imploring look, filled with doubt and unbelief. The voice which answered was low and slow.

"I don't know what I mean, Rogan, but you can never make me think Henry Spicer would steal those items. That he would commit murder and suicide seems impossible."

Rogan's lips parted to allow a sudden outburst of words, then closed. His eyes found the button on the desk, with a bang his big hand went slamming down on its top. Again and again the motion was repeated.

By his side Manners stood thinking. The letter he had read bore in one corner the engraved address of the library. But he knew Henry Spicer; everyone in the city knew him. Genial and friendly to the general public, he was well known to a smaller circle as one of the best informed men in his field in the country. A happy sort of a man, kindly to those who were under him, one who laughed a great deal oftener than he frowned. That he should be dead by his own hand was incredible.

The door from the hallway was jerked open and a police lieutenant came running into the room. The man's face wore a puzzled expression as if he was not accustomed to being summoned so vigorously by his superior officer. Long before he reached the desk, commands were being barked at him from the chief's lips.

"Have the police ambulance go to the old Hunt place at once. Take Bell, the fingerprint man, if you can find him. Send someone over to the library for Kent if he is not in his office. And get busy."

Though the man was without doubt puzzled by the fact, there was no explanation needed. He nodded.

"It will be about ten minutes before we can use the ambulance," he said. "It's out on an accident." Growling out a command to use it as soon as it returned, Rogan ordered him out of the office. As the door shut, the chief reached down to the desk and yanked open a drawer. A handful of stogies went into his pocket. His hat was thrust upon his head, then he hesitated. Again a hand went to a drawer and Manners glimpsed the black, squatty revolver which was thrust into an outside pocket.

"Where is your car, Harley?"

Told it was at a garage a block away, Rogan started for the door with a command to the professor to hurry. They were out on the street in a moment, hastening up the block and into the garage. The sight of the police chief caused the attendant to have the car on the floor almost before the request had left Manners' lips. He remembered as he drove out on the street, that in his haste he had forgotten to pay for his parking.

There had been a command whispered in his ear, an injunction to hurry. He slid around a traffic sign, and an indignant officer yelled at him as he went past. Weaving through slow-moving cars, paying no attention to lights or street cars, the big blue machine went dashing up the principal street of the city. Traffic policeman started to blow their whistles, only to snatch them suddenly from their lips as they glimpsed the blue-coated figure at Manners' side. The Hunt estate, the note had read. This was on the farther outskirts of the city, several acres of rundown land which had been without a tenant for a number of years. Once it had been the show place of the state, but that was many years ago. Now behind the high stone wall which enclosed the estate lay a tangled jungle of small trees and shrubbery. In a sense the place was an eyesore, neglected, desolate and lonely. The nearest house was over half a mile from the deserted brick dwelling which once had cost a fortune.

Though Manners was driving over fifty, yet as he left the main part of the city he allowed the tiny needle on the speedometer to creep around sixtyfive. The chief was in a hurry, wishing to reach the place before the other police officials arrived on the scene. There would be no difficulty in doing that. With his eyes glued to the flying road ahead, Manners was thinking. Beside him, slumped far down in his seat, with one hand holding his hat on his head, was the chief. Not a word had passed his lips since the command to hasten. There was no need to look at his face. Manners knew what the look would reveal, a hard expression, with lips set in a straight firm line, eyes narrow and steel gray.

They were going almost seventy miles an hour, rushing wildly over the streets of the city in order to be the first to see Spicer's body. Spicer had been almost a close friend of Manners', a man he admired, whose wit and good humor had often caused him to laugh. Now he was dead. Dead, said the rushing wheels. Dead, whistled the wind. Dead by his own hand in his own car. Manners knew that he did not believe the last.

They were running down a wide avenue, with wide lawns and costly houses, where children paused to watch the car flash by, and dogs, after one desperate attempt to follow, turned and ran barking to the sidewalk. Now came smaller streets, with rough, uneven pavement, where the machine rocked and swayed as it pounded along. A dirt road at last, turning at a sudden angle to run up the steep hill which towered above them.

Though the section of the city they had just left was respectable enough, yet it was a place of small frame houses and narrow lots. As the car started to bump up the hill, the houses vanished and on each side of the narrow road stretched fields overgrown with tall grass. Above them the road disappeared over the top of the hill.

The road they were climbing was extremely narrow, deeply rutted and covered with thick dust. Evidently it was not used much. Manners knew that there was another approach to the Hunt estate, but this was the nearest, and though the road just before cresting the top rose above them at a twentyfive percent angle, the car made it easily.

On the summit he turned to the left to follow what might far better have been called a path than a road. It ran through a field, and the grass was almost to the top of the car door. Only two narrow lanes showed where other machines had gone, and these were rather faint. Passing the field, they went through a small woods to come out along a stone wall.

It was a tall wall, over seven feet in height, built of heavy granite blocks. Someone must have spent a fortune upon this wall, for it ran around what was known as the Hunt estate. To see over its top was impossible, though they could glimpse the trees which were on the other side. For over a thousand yards they followed it, stopping before a rusty iron gate.

The gate which led through the wall had once been wrought by hands skilled in artistic workmanship. Even now, though rust from the rains of many years had corroded the fine lines of the iron, it still bore traces of beauty. Through it they could look into the grounds, see the tangled mass of trees on each side of a road which curved out of their vision.

Manners stepped out of the car. Hastening across the grass, he tried the rusty catch of the gate. With a protesting creak it moved as he swung the heavy sections aside. Back in the car, he threw in the clutch and they started through the walls.

The sunken garden, the note had said. Manners knew where the garden lay. Several times he had walked through the estate, wondering why it was that a place which held such possibilities of beauty had been allowed to fall into decay. The sunken garden was near the house, almost in the very center of the grounds. All they had to do to reach it was to follow the rough road winding through the trees.

On each side of the car was a tree-covered underbrush of neglected meadow. Once this had been kept in good condition. Years had passed since anyone had lived on the place, and the small shrubbery and trees had overrun the fields. Now they were a tangled thicket of vines and shrubs, so thickly grown together that one would find it difficult to pass through them.

They could not go fast for the road leading between the tangle of trees was covered with small branches and high grass. Reaching a curve they swept around it and saw ahead of them a large brick house. It was half hidden by high elm trees, and the windows appeared to be covered with boards. The sunken garden was on the other side of the house.

The path curved past a wooden barn; they saw that the door was off, lying half hidden in the weeds. The vague outlines of a garden were passed; then came the side of the house, a large house, desolate and lonely in appearance, with its windows covered with boards, dirty with the dust of years. Past the house they found they could go no farther, for the road turned off in another direction.

It had been a silent ride, neither Rogan nor Manners saying a word. As the car came to a stop, and the sound of the engine died away, the chief stirred to attention. With a jerk he pulled his heavy body upright, to cast an uneasy glance over what had been a lawn. At the lower edge of the tall grass he saw the sunken garden and beyond it, half hidden by the unkempt hedge, a parked car.

His hand reached forth to fall heavily upon Manners' arm. A finger pointed over the high grass. Turning, the professor followed the gesture, his face becoming stern as he saw the car. Only the rear end of it could be seen, but he knew the dark blue machine. The car standing motionless at the farther end of the sunken garden belonged to Henry Spicer.

Not a word was said as they hastened out on the ground and started through the grass. Weeds plucked at their feet, small branches from the trees above their heads tried to trip them. Over what had been a wide lawn they hastened, skirting the sunken garden, now a mass of weeds mingled with golden rod.

Beyond the sunken garden a field stretched to an overgrown and unkempt privet hedge. Once the hedge must have been a thing of beauty; now it was a green mass of tangled branches. In the center was a wide opening, filled with grass and weeds. Here was the blue coupe, standing with its back toward the house.

As he walked toward the hedge, the grass swishing against his legs, a shiver of dread swept over Manners' body. Far away could be heard the noisy quarreling of a flock of crows. Around him was sunshine, playing over the ruin and decay. In such a setting the blue machine took on the appearance of some threatening thing.

When they passed the opening in the hedge, the footsteps of the two men slackened. There was reluctance in their manner as they approached the rear of the car. Neither spoke, nor did they turn their eyes to look upon each other's faces. The same thought was in both minds, a dread of what they would see when they looked within the machine.

It was Rogan whose hand fell upon the handle of the door. Very slow was the motion of turning, slower yet the motion of pulling the door open. There came a quick look within, then the heavy, thick-set figure stiffened.

Turning, he threw a horrified look at Manners, his lips were a stern, straight line.

Slumped down across the wheel, with one hand lying below the level of the seat, crouched the silent figure of a man. Over the car played the bright sunshine and the song of birds came floating from the trees. The figure within the car could not hear the birds, knew nothing about the warm sunlight. Whatever might happen in the world he had loved, Henry Spicer would never know. For him the world no longer existed.

Without speaking they stood for several moments, studying the silent figure slumped down upon the seat. Death might be a dignified thing, but there was nothing dignified about the body lying over the steering wheel. Instead, there was a grotesque appearance of mockery, a sense of futility which the bright sunshine could not dispel. Spicer in life had been a cheerful soul, laughing at the comedy he found about him. In death his body had become a sinister thing of horror.

With a sigh Rogan bent forward to lift the cold hand which dangled below the seat level. For a moment he held it in his palm, his hand looking at the automatic revolver clenched between the cold stiff fingers. Carefully letting the arm drop he turned to Manners.

"The gun is there, and if you look you can see the wound, a little over his temple."

Pushing the chief to one side Manners bent forward to study the interior of the machine. The lining of the seat was of heavy velvet, and he glanced at this for a moment. Bending forward he looked at the cold face, studying the wound which was a little over the eye. His hand reached down to touch the gun, then for a little while did not stir.

When he turned away from the machine it was to look around him. Behind them was the opening in the hedge leading to the neglected lawn. In front of the car was a vague track, curving away through the small trees to vanish in the distance. To reach the place where the car was standing, it must have been driven over this indistinct path.

The silence was broken by the sound of an approaching car. It was somewhere to their left, the noise of the engine drifting through the tangle of small trees. With his head bent on one side, Rogan listened a moment, then reaching into his pocket found his police whistle. Applying it to his lips, he blew three sharp long blasts, which were answered in a second.

The whistle was blown many times before anyone came in sight. Then they saw three men walking around the side of the garden, hurrying men, with the tall figure of the inspector of the homicide squad in the lead. Observing them, Kent gave a wave of his hand.

There was curiosity upon the inspector's face as he came toward the hedge. Though Rogan had ordered the police ambulance sent to the Hunt estate, he had said nothing as to the reason for the request. That Kent should wonder what had taken place was not surprising, and an astonished look swept over his face as he saw them standing beside the blue coupe. He was half way through the hedge before he spoke:

"What's the matter, chief?"

A stogie came out of the chief's pocket. The end was bitten off, the match applied before he answered. With a wave of his hand toward the coupe he uttered a short sentence:

"Spicer is in there, dead."

As Kent suddenly halted, the two men who were with him reached his side. One was the young police doctor, the other the patrolman who drove the ambulance. The doctor did not pause. Hearing Rogan's remark, he walked past the inspector and pulled open the door by the wheel. They saw him hesitate for a second, then his head and shoulders vanished from sight.

With a look at Rogan the inspector hastened to the other door to assist the physician. As the tall back bent within the car, Rogan walked to the front of the car. His eyes were going down the narrow outlined path, turning in the end to take in the tangle of trees on both sides of the machine. In his pocket was the letter which told him he would find Spicer's body at this place. When he read it there had been two thoughts in his mind. The first was surprise, the astonished wonder that the librarian should have been the one who had stolen the pamphlets and committed the murder. His second thought had been one of relief. Spicer had confessed, confessed in the most convincing manner, by taking his own life. The confession ended the case.

Now as his eyes took in the warm landscape, he felt very uneasy. He tried to tell himself that there was nothing to cause the feeling. Spicer had confessed; the letter was in his pocket; the man was dead. But deep down in his heart he was wondering. Intuition was again at work, warning him that things were not just what they seemed, whispering that he must be careful, must not jump at conclusions.

The sound behind him caused the heavy figure to whirl around. The doctor and Kent had walked to the front of the car. The blond head of the physician was nodding in agreement with something the inspector was saying. Yet for some reason, Rogan decided the nod was not as vigorous as he would have liked to see.

"What do you think?" he called out. "Oh, I guess he just croaked himself. But why under heaven Spicer should do a thing like that—" and the doctor shook his head as though words were beyond him.

Crossing to their side Rogan's hand went searching into his pocket; the fingers closed upon a piece of paper and he brought it forth. For a moment his eyes looked at the single sheet, saw the typewritten letters which announced that a well-known citizen had died by his own hand. Then he extended it to Kent.

"Here is a letter from him. It's the thing which brought us here to find his body."

A quick questioning look at his superior and the inspector's hand shot forth for the letter. As he bent his eyes to the page, the doctor crowded close to look over his shoulder. Silence for a moment, a gasp, then an excited remark:

"Who would have thought it, chief? That ends the thing. Who would have thought it?"

Manners' eyes went searching into the gloomy interior of the car. There was a frown upon his face, and he was biting his lips. The glance traveled over the silent figure, and for a moment he did not speak. Then he moved; the voice which spoke was very slow:

"Chief, did you look at the postmark on that letter?"

There came a shake of the white head as his hand shot into his pocket. When he saw the envelope Manners turned to the doctor.

"How long would you say he has been dead, Trent?"

"Anywhere from sixteen to eighteen hours."

"That's what I thought," was the dry retort.

Something in the deliberate tone caused Rogan to lift his eyes from the envelope, to look doubtfully at his friend. There had been a curious undertone in the retort, a mixture of irony playing with a troubled doubt. Something was on Manners' mind, something which had caused his friend's face to become suddenly very grave.

"What are you getting at?"

"This. There are three things about this car which look very funny to me. And—"

He paused, as there came a sharp barking question from the chief.

"What in hell are you trying to tell?"

There was no reply for a moment. In the silence they heard a cat-bird in a near-by tree break into a harsh cry. Somewhere a car sounded a horn, its shrill echo floating to their ears. As it died away Manners spoke:

"It's not suicide, Rogan. It's murder. Your second murder in the library affair."

CHAPTER FOURTEEN

Rogan stood looking at a tiny cloud, a cloud which in a moment would become part of the blue mist of the sky. Observers seeing his face might have wondered why he had such an interest in the sky. They would not know that his eyes, though they were fixed upon the cloud, did not notice it; that his gaze was that of a man trying to get his thoughts in order.

A warning feeling of intuition had swept over him when he first glimpsed the silent figure in the car. It was a feeling he could not classify, nor could he tell what caused it, but it was one which he respected. There had been other occasions when that same intuition had warned him to be careful, times when he had felt just as he did at the present moment.

"Harley," he asked, "what makes you say a thing like that?"

"Did you observe what Spicer was wearing?"

"His glad rags," was the retort.

"You found him dead in his car, wearing a tuxedo. Where is his top coat? Spicer would not drive without it, wearing dinner clothes. Can you think of a person about to commit suicide putting on a dinner jacket and then driving miles to kill himself on a lonely, deserted estate? If you can, it's something I cannot. What hour is stamped on that envelope?"

"One o'clock," was the admission.

"One o'clock. When do you think that letter was mailed? Spicer has been dead for at least sixteen hours, Trent says. You know as well as I do that if that letter had been mailed anywhere in the city last night it would have been delivered to you around eight o'clock. They pick mail up from every box in the city at six in the morning. The letter was not mailed last night."

Hastily drawing the envelope from his pocket, Rogan gave it a hurried look. In the upper corner was a circle with the hour stamped within. It said one o'clock as plainly as possible. What was more, he knew Manners was right. There was an early morning collection of mail at six o'clock. If it had been picked up then, the letter would have been on his desk when he entered the office.

"It looks queer," he commenced, only to have the words taken out of his mouth.

"Of course it's queer. You know darned well if Spicer committed suicide he must have posted that letter before killing himself. That would be sometime last night. If he had posted it, the letter would have been picked up this morning at six. That letter was mailed this morning, and that means that Spicer never mailed it."

Kent felt moved to break into the argument. "It could have been given to someone to mail, someone who was told not to mail it until morning."

But as he said this he did not believe it. Nor did Manners accept the theory. He admitted that it was possible; it might have been done, though he stated very positively that he did not believe it. With irony in his voice he reminded them that inside the car was Spicer, dressed in dinner clothes. Did the average man who committed suicide dress before taking his life? Did he drive through the city streets in dinner clothes without wearing a top coat? Would Spicer, above all other men, do this?

An uneasy silence had come over the three police officials. Rogan knew that when he had remarked that the case was over, he had not believed what he said. As for Kent, he did not know what to think. The usual details of police work found in him an officer whose superior was hard to find, but he lacked imagination and his mind could not easily jump to the conclusions the professor was reaching. Having nothing to say, he kept silent.

"That's all right, Prof," came Trent's voice, "but you sure have got to have more than that to make me think it's not suicide."

The look the physician received caused him to wonder if he had not spoken too soon. Without a word, Manners took two steps, his long arms reaching out for the doctor's coat. The grip which fell upon Trent's shoulder was firm, and the astonished young man was pulled to the side of the machine, his head thrust through the open door.

"Look carefully, Trent, at both Spicer's eyes and at the manner in which his hand holds that gun."

There was irony behind that dry tone, a faint hint of sarcasm which caused the doctor to look around and give one quick, searching look at the professor. The stern expression around the tightly closed lips caused him to turn, and they watched his shoulders disappear within the car. It was almost five minutes before the head was withdrawn and his first action was to look at Manners, then gravely nod his head.

"What the devil are you two—" began the rough voice of the chief. The question was never finished, for a gesture from Manners caused him to become silent.

"Chief, if you will look at Spicer's eyes you will find them tight shut. Yet if there is one bit of medical evidence we are certain of, it is that when a person meets a violent death, or one which comes suddenly, you will always find the eyes wide open. In cases where death comes slowly they are generally half open, never tight shut."

Rogan stared at his friend as if he believed he had suddenly gone crazy. When he started to speak the first words came in a low tone, but the voice rose as he went on.

"Well, if when a man kills himself or gets bumped off his eyes are the same, I don't see what difference it makes. A sudden startled look swept his face, the big jaw dropped for a second to allow one word to burst forth, "Hell."

"That's the right word, Rogan. Spicer's eyes are closed, shut tight. If he committed suicide they would be open, staring straight ahead, and the same if it was murder. Now we are not sure about the murder end, but we do know his eyes are closed. Someone slipped up. Someone thought the eyes of every dead person should be shut tight and, seeing Spicer's were open, closed them. Ask Trent."

There was a sheepish expression upon the doctor's face. The first glance he had given the body was a casual one, observing the wound above the right eye, glancing at the gun held in the hand. The fact that the eyes-were closed he had overlooked. Manners was right, the eyes should have been open and in a grave voice he admitted that his examination had been careless.

Brushing by the two men, Kent thrust his head into the car. The gesture was that of a man who would refuse to believe what had been said until the evidence of his own eyes convinced him. When the head was withdrawn, the look he threw at his chief was a convincing one. Then he turned to Manners.

"What else have you got?"

"The gun. Do you think the grip of the hand which holds the gun is a firm one? It is, in a sense, but not firm enough. In a suicide case, one from shooting, a muscular spasm follows the shot, which causes the hand to grip the gun so tightly that it is almost impossible to loosen the clasp. Most medicolegal works tell us that a gun clasped firmly, the grip caused by the muscular reaction, is the best evidence of suicide. Now that gun is in Spicer's hand, but it can be moved. Not very much it is true, but far more than would be possible if he had shot himself. It's my idea the revolver was placed in his hand after death and the fingers forced around the gun. I think Trent will agree with me."

A quick glance at his doctor, and Rogan saw the young man nod. Then the chief turned to look up the path and for a moment seemed to be studying the tall grass. When he whirled around there was a little irony in his voice.

"Got anything else we overlooked?"

"Yes. Several other things are worth considering.There are hardly any powder marks on his face, and there should be. If he held that gun in his hand and shot himself, no matter how far away he held it, there would be a slight burn. There is none. What's more I don't think Spicer was killed in this spot. You see chief, I knew Spicer, and I know darned well he would not steal those pamphlets or kill himself. And of course I don't believe he wrote the note you got."

"What sense was there in anyone killing him and then writing me a note saying where I could find the body?"

"There's your entire motive, Rogan. What does the note say? That Spicer stole the pamphlets, killed Ruby Merton because she had discovered what he had done, then killed himself because the police were getting close. If you believed all that, the case was over. Someone wanted you to believe the case was closed."

"But we are not getting close," was Kent's protest.

Manners agreed with the remark. He added that it would have been only a matter of days before they discovered that the pamphlets had been stolen. He did not believe, though he did not say so, that the police would have made the discovery. They knew nothing about early Americana, and their rare value—that is, unless someone told them. Rare books and the prices paid for them were outside of their knowledge.

Rogan glanced at his two assistants, though he knew what the look would reveal. Trent's face was a study, chagrin and excitement playing across the thin features. Kent seemed startled, but was saying nothing. Behind them, looking very doubtfully at the car, stood the patrolman, and as his eyes rested on the blue uniform the chief swept into action.

"Can you drive the ambulance over here, Mike?" He was assured it could be done, though the big car would have to be driven carefully over the grass. He snapped out the quick command, then he turned to Manners.

"It's a good bet you are right," he said. "If you are, then the odds are against his having been killed here. Someone shot him, then drove the car to this place and left it. Let's give a look down that path. There's no other place they could have driven from. This car could not have gone through the hedge."

As the three police authorities started to examine the ground, Manners turned to thrust his head again into the machine. His eyes rested for a moment upon the grotesque figure sprawled across the wheel, passed down to the hand which held the gun, swept over the shining instrument board. Then he gave a start. There was no key in the ignition lock.

His eyes narrowed as he saw this. If Spicer had shot himself, one would hardly expect he would bother to place the key in his pocket after turning off the engine. Going to the other side of the machine, he opened the door, and, though he did not like his task, thrust his fingers into the small pocket of Spicer's vest, then into the trousers. The search was useless; there was no key; nor did he find it on the floor of the machine.

But he did discover something else. Tucked half under the floor mat was a small bit of paper. It was the back of an envelope, folded in the middle, either cast aside as useless or fallen unnoticed to the floor. There was nothing of interest upon it. One side was covered with a mass of small circles, drawn again and again on one side of the paper. What it could mean he did not try to find out. Just a series of circles, starting with a small one, then others larger in size drawn around the first. After a short look he placed it in his pocket.

Withdrawing his head, he saw the men some distance down the faint path. Let them go; he would look over the machine. By the time he had ended his search the men were back at his side, and through the hedge could be heard the approaching rumble of the ambulance. He had discovered nothing and he doubted if Rogan had.

He was informed that they were certain the machine had been driven over the path, and that the tracks turned in the distance to join a road. This road came in on the other side of the estate. The grass was matted down in several places and there were several impressions of tires. There was no doubt the machine had come from that direction.

The ambulance had reached the hedge; the driver was climbing down from his seat. Leaving the engine running, he came to the side of the coupe, casting a questioning look at his chief, a look which caused Rogan to frown. After studying the landscape he spoke:

"Mike, you and Trent take the body down to the morgue. I am going to have Kent drive Spicer's machine back. I want that car looked over carefully. Fingerprint everything. I will go back with Manners. Meet you all in the office later."

With a motion to Manners, he started to hasten towards the opening in the hedge. The professor's remark caused him to whirl around.

"There's no key in the ignition switch, and it's not in Spicer's clothes."

With a shrug of his shoulders, Rogan pondered over the new information. If the key was not in the switch, could not be found in the car, Manners was right. Not only had Spicer been murdered, but the crime had taken place elsewhere. Turning, he told the patrolman to go to a garage, get a key then come back for the coupe.

Nodding toward his inspector, he started to walk toward the sunken garden. He was thinking over the new fact. Every fact, no matter how insignificant, must be investigated. However, it would now be possible to use ordinary police methods. A visit to the club where Spicer lived was the next step. They climbed into the car without speaking and, after lighting a stogie, Rogan slumped far down into his seat. When they came through the stone walls he could have observed the most beautiful view in the city, but his eyes never rested upon it. Views never meant much to Rogan, now he would not have raised his head for the finest view in the world. There was work ahead, a great deal of work, also a good deal of criticism to face. The city would rock with horror when they heard what had happened.

The car stopped before a large brick building and almost before it stopped Rogan had tumbled out. It was the Waveland Club, the most exclusive social group of the city. As he followed the chief past a startled doorman, Manners decided to eat. It was time he did this, and there was no more convenient place than his own club. With a word to Rogan, he left him talking to the secretary and turned into the dining room.

He gave his order and then leaned back to light a cigarette. The dining room was quiet, for he had it all to himself. On every side were small tables, the linen snow white, the silver gleaming. Over the room hung a deep silence, the silence one finds in churches and in many exclusive clubs. He half smiled as he thought of the excitement which would sweep over the place in a few moments.

Spicer had lived here. He was unmarried. His suite had been on the top floor of the building, one of the ten suites the club possessed. Here the professional leaders of the city's life came for quiet and companionship. Not a very exciting club, but one whose respectability had never been touched with scandal. Well, it would be now.

He thought of the dead librarian. There were few men who had known their profession better than Spicer. He had loved his work, loved everything which had to do with books. Of course anyone in a public position had critics, and there were those who did not like the librarian. One could not be liked by everyone, but that he had any real enemies was absurd.

Spicer the one who had taken the pamphlets from the safe? No. There were some things certain types of people never did. The pamphlets were the most valuable possession of the library; to the librarian they would be almost like a child. Psychologically it would have been impossible for Spicer to have stolen them. He was not the type to do such a thing. As for the letter which confessed murdering Ruby Merton, Spicer had never written that.

All through his lunch, he pondered over the letter. It was a confession, but not that of Spicer. Instead it was the actual confession of the murderer, whoever that might be. It was true that Spicer would not have taken the pamphlets, but a much greater certainty was that he would never commit murder. As for killing himself, that was impossible. Manners had reached that conclusion when the meal ended.

The clerk in the office told him that Rogan was in Spicer's apartment. It was clear from the bewildered expression upon the man's face that he wished to ask what the police chief was doing. Police and the Waveland Club were two things which had nothing in common. Not only was the clerk curious, but he appeared shocked that a blue uniform should have invaded the sacred places of the building.

Taking the elevator, Manners went to the top floor and came out in a deeply carpeted hallway. Standing for a moment in heavy silence, he heard the elevator descend. He had spent several evenings in the librarian's suite, nights of enjoyment, which now were over. His hand touched a mahogany door, he sadly shook his head.

Turning the knob he stepped into a large living room. Bookcases lined one side of the wall, with colored prints and etchings above them. It was a room bearing signs of quiet culture, whose furnishings were in the best of taste. Through an open door he glimpsed a bedroom, saw Rogan bending over a dresser. Inside the room he noticed first that the bed had not been slept in, or, if it had, was now remade.

At his approach the chief whirled around.

"Harley, they told me downstairs Spicer was playing bridge in the card room last night. Some time around nine-thirty he got a telephone call, came back and said he had to go out. Was a little excited when he left, told them he would be back in an hour. He never came back."

"Didn't say who the call was from, or what it was about?"

Very profane was the reply. Manners could see that Rogan's nerves were getting the better of him. The voice that told of the telephone call was not only rough it was also a bit angry. Spicer had said nothing about his message, giving no hint whom it was from, nor what it was about. He had asked that his car be brought to the front of the club. When he left he said he would be back in an hour.

"He was excited they say. Of course we will look up the men with whom he was playing cards, try to trace the call; but there is not much chance in doing that. Anyway something dragged him out of the club."

"To his death, Rogan."

At his words the heavy figure straightened and after a moment walked over to the window. There was dejection in the way he slumped down in a chair. When he spoke the voice was weary, plaintive in its tone.

"I guess you are right, Harley. Looks like it. What a hell of a case. First the woman, then Rand, now Spicer. How the city will rock when the papers get out on the street! And there is not much to go on."

"You have, however, a complete series of events now. Starting with the stealing of the pamphlets, you go directly to the murder of the woman, then to the assault on Rand, ending with the death of Spicer. They are all connected; all have the same motive." There came the slow nod of Rogan's white head as he said the one word, "Fear."

"Fear, of course. Fear of exposure. A fear which drives some excited persons to believe they can cover a wrong by killing those who know."

"Harley, do you think Spicer knew who killed the Merton woman?"

Did Spicer know? That question had been playing through Manners' mind for the last hour. From one angle it might appear that he did, that his murderer might know of his knowledge. Yet he was not so certain.

"Rogan," he confessed, "I don't know. I believe the message which came to Spicer over the telephone may have hinted that he would be told who killed his reference librarian. What is more, it's my idea that he knew the person who called. I cannot picture Spicer going out on a wild call over the wire, not knowing the person he was going to see."

"There were fourteen gallons of gas in that machine," was the unexpected reply. "He must have had it filled when he took it to the garage. Wherever he went, it was not so far away. You only get about ten miles a gallon with those big boats. No matter where he was killed he did not go more than eight or ten miles from here."

It was a new thought and one that would have to be looked into. As Manners thought this, there came a knock at the door. Rogan's voice called out for the person to enter. As the door was being opened there came a request from the official. It was not directed to Manners, simply the expression of a deep wish within the chief's heart.

"I wish I knew the kind of a person who would pull off these crazy killings."

Manners did not watch his friend cross the floor and bark out his commands to the three plain-clothes men who entered. An idea was sweeping over him. It was not a new thought, though he had not given it much attention before. Now he realized that it was very much worth considering, decided perhaps it was the only thing which promised any solution of the crimes. Thinking this, he gave a violent start as he turned and hurried out of the living room.

Beside a table covered with books and magazines, Rogan was barking out instructions to three of the homicide squad. Bellboys were to be examined, clerks talked with, the telephone calls traced, the garage visited. One man must get into touch with the banks, discover how Spicer's account stood. Work was ahead, the hard work in which details must be taken care of. The chief was going into action.

As for Manners, he was now longing for the quiet of his own living room. He could see the long, booklined walls, picture the sunlight streaming in through the open windows. Up on the hill there was peace and quiet. These were the things he needed very badly. An idea was shaping itself, an idea which would need careful consideration. He would go home, in the restful quietness of his book-lined room, think over what had come to him.

CHAPTER FIFTEEN

Bathed in a flood of warm sunlight, the lawn stretched away to an ivy-covered wall. A fat robin hopped slowly around the front of the garden, pausing to look up to the tall young man seated under a great elm. For over an hour the robin had been interested in the silent figure, and one might have said the little beady eyes which darted toward the chair were filled with curiosity.

With his legs stretched before him, Harley Manners gazed reflectively over his domain. To his right was his rambling house, its side covered with late roses. Under the windows stretched a long narrow garden, colorful against the vivid green of the lawn. Above him towered the tall elms, casting deep shadows over the grass. By his side, keeping one watchful eye upon the robin, lay the Airedale, ready to rise at the least suggestion.

For the last hour and a half, with a pencil in his hand, a block of paper in his lap, Manners had been writing. There had been no particular order to his notes, simply the jotting down of random ideas which had flashed through his mind, thoughts all having some connection with the two murders.

When he placed the papers aside, he doubted if the time had been well spent. There was something he should remember, some little fact which up to now had escaped his notice. The random jotting down of his thoughts had been an attempt to arouse a train of association. Some little incident was trying to force its way through his subconscious. So far, the effort had been a failure.

By turning his head, he could have seen a faint haze upon the air. Down in the city the smoke from the factories would die away in a short while. Twilight was approaching; a hush was creeping through the trees, becoming part of the shadows upon the grasses. Soon it would be night. He had promised Rogan to call at the police station at ten.

Down in the city a well-functioning police machinery was now at work. Men would be scurrying round trying to discover some fact which would throw light upon Spicer's death. Though at first the chief had wished to think it was suicide, he had been forced to admit that another violent death had taken place, one which might be as difficult to solve as the first. Reaching down, Manners picked up the papers containing his notes. Page after page of yellow paper was filled with his oddly characteristic writing. Line after line ended in a black question mark. He smiled as he turned the sheets to see that almost every line ended with this symbol.

Of one thing he was very certain, the death of the woman, the assault upon the reporter, the murder of Spicer were in a sense one crime, a crime which up to the present had three chapters. Which chapter might be the most important he did not know, though he was inclined to think it was the first. The death of the woman was the first circle, the other events were contained within it.

Rogan had said that as a rule there were but three motives for crime: greed, revenge, and the various vagaries of sexual background. He had remarked that none of the usual motives could be suspected in this case. When Manners had agreed with Rogan, it had appeared very evident that the police chief was correct. He was not so certain now.

Greed, the desire for money. The three pamphlets which had been stolen, they could be sold for at least eleven thousand dollars in any book-auction room. The first murder never would have been committed if the pamphlets had not been stolen. So greed, desire for money, was one of the motives in the crime.

Revenge? No, they would have to rule that out. But there was a motive just as important as the others: Fear. Fear played a great part in many crimes. His bookcases were filled with stories of famous crimes, in which the driving impulse had been fear. Fear of the consequences of some act, fear of exposure. Fear explained the death of the woman. Someone was afraid of what she might say.

Sex, as a motive seemed impossible. Ruby Merton was over sixty, no thought of sex could play around her. Yet there was an uneasy thought in Manners' mind. They had dismissed all the usual motives, now they were certain that greed and fear played a part.

It might be that, instead of none of the usual motives playing a part, they would discover in the end that this case contained them all. One sheet of the yellow paper met his eye. It bore but a single word written in big sprawling letters.

"Type" was the word, and after it was a long black question mark. For the last hour this word had been present in his mind. What sort of an individual would steal the pamphlets? For the person who had stolen them must have committed the two murders. Always Manners approached the problem from the psychological angle. Not who committed a crime, but what type of individual would be guilty? Find that out and to discover who it was would be a comparatively easy task.

Only a book collector, familiar with the value of rare books, could have known that the pamphlets were worth eleven thousand dollars. Once the entire city had been told the library possessed the books. That, however, was nine years ago. Everyone knew about them then, but what everybody knows is soon forgotten.

The library staff would know they were in the safe, but they would not be very much interested in the safe or its contents. When the day's work was over, books were the last thing they wished to see. Who, outside of the library staff, could have been interested in the pamphlets? For someone had been. There were three book collectors worthy of the name in the city, two, if he did not count himself. One, however, was interested only in items dealing with the theater and early English sporting books. This man would not turn his head to look at Americana. The other—and he smiled as he thought of the leading physician of the city, a man whose collection of early medical works was the best in the country.

No book collector he had ever heard of would stoop to murder. He chuckled, however, at a thought, remembering the typical French case, of a book collector who killed a rival, then burned his house in order to be the only possessor of a book. The smile was caused by the ironical recollection, that, after the man had committed his crime, he discovered that the book was worthless.

Yet he was right, book collectors did not steal from libraries. The chief requisite for being a collec-tor was a well-filled pocket book. The rare items had been stolen, but he was certain they were not resting upon the shelves of any collector in the city. They had been taken for the price they would bring.

This presented another difficulty. Whoever had stolen the pamphlets had to be one who knew something about their value. He must also possess knowledge of the markets for such things. This sort of knowledge was technical, not known to the average person. The three items were worth almost eleven thousand dollars, but one would have to know where they could be sold.

Dismissing this thought, he tried to repicture the first murder. The pamphlets had been stolen, the librarian had discovered that they were not in the safe. The discovery must have been made the morning of her death. It would explain her nervous, excited condition, the frantic attempts to telephone on a line which was out of order. It would explain another fact.

She knew who had taken the pamphlets. There seemed no doubt she had been trying to reach the individual she suspected. Why should she try to see him instead of giving her information to the police? If she was certain who had taken them, the police would have been the logical ones to call in.

Two things might have prevented that action.

Spicer had been away, but would be at the library by noon. During the afternoon she had tried to see him. He was busy. That, coupled with the fact that she was a bit of a bore, had prevented her getting into his office. She would not wish to take any action until her superior had been consulted.

There were other considerations. She had an idea who the guilty person was, but there was a hint that she had not cared to be over hasty in what she did.

Was this caused by the social standing of the person accused? If Manners was correct in his thinking, she had called the person she suspected on the telephone, perhaps invited him to come into the office and talk the matter over. It seemed logical.

When Rogan first glanced at the letter, he was convinced that Spicer, by taking his life, had confessed to the murder. But if there was one thing of which Manners was positive, it was that Spicer knew nothing about the crime. No one who had known the head of the library would ever believe the letter was anything but a forgery.

Who had killed Ruby Merton? This he did not know, though he was certain it was the same individual who had murdered Spicer. The last had been a skillfully planned crime, one which had required a cool head. Spicer could not have been killed at the place where they found his body; the murder had been committed elsewhere. As he thought this a picture came flashing through his mind.

Spicer had been killed at the place he visited after receiving the telephone message. The call had been unexpected; the librarian had at once ordered his car and hastily left the club. They would discover that he had not intended to leave the building that evening. His dinner jacket showed that he had dressed for a bridge party.

A message had called him out of his club to his death. Manners shuddered as he pictured the murderer driving along a dark road with the body of his victim slumped down on the seat beside him. That required nerve, a cool taking of chances which no ordinary man would face. He could see the blue coupe with its sinister burden, driving past lighted cars, turning at last into the Hunt estate, coming to a halt at last by the garden. But the letter the chief had received bothered him.

Scotland Yard had once said that there were ten clues to every murder. Perhaps to the highly trained department of the Yard that might be so, though he rather doubted it. One thing was certain, there had never been a crime, no matter how skillfully planned, in which the murderer did not overlook something. In this case it was the letter.

The letter had but one purpose, to make the chief of police believe its contents were true. If this could be done the case was closed; the murderer was safe. But he had made a mistake. The letter had been posted some hours after Spicer's death. If Spicer had written it, he would have mailed it before he left the hotel. Mailed after death, it showed very clearly that the murderer himself had posted it. What type of individual could be guilty of the two deaths? This had bothered Manners all afternoon. Intelligent people did not as a rule commit crime; when they did, it was in a moment of emotional frenzy. There were hints of emotional unbalance in the two murders, emotions whipped into a wild excitement by fear of exposure. An individual whose mind was on the verge of breaking could have committed the murders.

He gave up thinking to reach into his pocket for a cigarette. As his fingers went searching into his pocket, they felt a piece of paper. Curiosity caused him to bring it forth. The back of an envelope was in his hand, its surface covered with circles which had been drawn with a pencil. His eyes narrowed as he glanced at the torn envelope. It had been on the floor of Spicer's machine, half hidden by the mat. He knew the meaning of the circles, why they had been drawn. The question who had drawn them was the important thing.

Why the circles had been drawn was easy to explain. Many persons when playing with a pencil begin unthinkingly to draw figures upon anything which is at hand. Their subconscious mind tricks them into always drawing the same design. Some people covered a telephone pad with drawings of heads; others drew little squares; every person had his own pattern.

The design upon the envelope was a simple thing. There would be a small circle, then around it another, then another, until the surface of the paper was covered. Something in the subconscious mind of the individual who had lost the paper had caused him to make the figures. Manners gave a start; only a few hours ago he had seen a similar design.

Down in the library, in the office where they had found the murdered woman was her desk. Across from where she had been sitting lay a pad of paper.

He remembered that the top of this pad was covered with circles, the same design as the envelope he had in his hand. As he thought this he rose to his feet to give a long low whistle.

Someone had sat in the chair across from the woman and, while sitting there, had unthinkingly drawn the figures upon the pad. The same figures had been found on the envelope picked up in the car.

It was too great a coincidence not to have some meaning. There was not one chance in a thousand that two persons would draw the same figures when playing with a pencil. Both murders had been committed by the same person.

A call came from the house, a voice saying that dinner would be served in a few moments. Calling the dog, he went over the grass, standing a moment by the door to take in the twilight. Then, going to his room, he washed and changed to a darker suit, and by the time he entered the dining room dinner was being served.

It was long after nine when he finished reading the paper, scowling a little at the account of the finding of

Spicer's body. From what he had read, he saw that Rogan had kept some facts from the press. There was no mention of the letter, nothing which hinted that Spicer must have been murdered.

All there was could have been put into a paragraph, though the story of the popular librarian's death covered two columns.

The wind had begun to come up after dark; he could hear the trees creaking upon the lawn. Rising, he crossed over to the bay window and throwing the curtains aside looked out at the night. There seemed every promise of a storm, with not a star to be seen. The only brightness which came to his eyes was the reflection from the street lights of the city lying below the hill.

With his face pressed close against the glass, he gazed through the window. The lawn was a dim place of moving shadows, which advanced and retreated with the swaying of the trees. He caught the vague shape of the garage, a dim etched outline at the farther edge of the lawn. Then all at once he darted back from the window, only to look carefully out again at the lawn.

As he had looked over the grass he thought there had been a vague moving figure which had suddenly darted to the shelter of the tree. It might have been fancy; perhaps it was only the shadow from one of the many trees. No one would be on his lawn, darting across his grass to hide beyond a tree. His eyes had deceived him. At this moment the telephone gave a shrill ring.

When he had lifted the receiver from the hook the voice which came over the wire caused wonder to leap in his mind, a low, soft voice, whose deliberation was remarkable because of the softness with which the words were being spoken. The voice asked twice if he was Professor Manners, hesitating before speaking another word.

As he waited for the low voice to speak again, Manners frowned. It was Zuko at the other end of the wire, and the gangster had never before called his house.

There was some reason for the call, and Joe was taking his own time in giving it. But after a pause the low slow voice came again.

"Still interested in libraries, Professor?" was the insinuating question.

The response made again, there came a long wait.

Whatever it was that Zuko was going to say, he not only was taking his time in saying it, but also was carefully picking his words. Again came the low voice:

"Professor, you had better be here, yes, at the Bagdad, by eleven. Might bring Rogan with you."

Before Manners could hurl an excited question into the telephone, he heard a faint click, knew that Zuko had rung off. Soberly he placed the receiver back on the hook, then stood thoughtfully looking down at the stand. Never before had Zuko called his house. The few words he had spoken over the telephone were not of much importance, what had caused the message was the chief thing.

Something was up. Zuko was a stickler for formalities. Was he still interested in libraries had been the question. If so, then he was to be at the Bagdad by eleven. Zuko had discovered something, and, as with a start, he rushed into the living room for the hat he had left upon the table, he knew the information he would receive at eleven did not concern the gangster. If it had, there would have been no low, insistent voice over the wire.

It was twenty minutes to the hour by the clock on the mantel. Just time enough to reach the police station at ten. He pictured Rogan's face when he told him Zuko's conversation, knew the argument he would have before he would be able to persuade the chief to go to the roadhouse. Rogan prided himself that his police department was clean. To make sure that it was kept clean, he had no dealings with Zuko. It was a far higher political power than Rogan possessed which kept the gangster out of jail.

With his hand upon the door leading out on the veranda, Manners paused for a second. The wind was rising and it might rain before he returned. Should he take a rain coat? Making up his mind not to do so, he flung the door half open, then decided that the coat had better be taken. At this thought he started to step behind the half opened door. It was this step which saved him.

As he turned away, the darkness was broken by a sharp, spitting dart of flame. Out of the silence came the ringing report of a gun. Something went smashing against the wall, and a picture fell with a crash to the floor. Out of the darkness of his lawn a shot had come hurtling through the place where he had stood only an instant before, a shot which had shattered the wall in his hallway.

CHAPTER SIXTEEN

Instinctively Manners' hand reached out for the door, slamming it shut with a bang which went resounding through the house. Pressed close against the wall, unable to move for a moment, he stood staring down at the picture lying upon the floor; a picture whose glass lay scattered in a hundred pieces. For a moment he stood there, then sprang into life. Two steps and his searching fingers found the light switch, and the hall was plunged into darkness; three more, and the lights in the living room were out. Now the entire house was in darkness, with not a light in any room. Groping through the dark living room, he found the desk and his hand pulled out a drawer. Somewhere in that drawer was a gun he wanted. Over rustling papers passed the searching fingers, sliding at last over a smooth, cold surface. The gun transferred to the pocket of his coat, he started for the kitchen.

His mind was still a mass of tangled emotions. Only the fact that he had started to turn back for his raincoat had saved him. Out on the dark lawn there had been a watching figure, waiting until he opened the door and stood outlined by the light within the hallway. But why should anyone wish to take his life?

The telephone call came surging into his mind, if he did not know Zuko it would bear all the details of a well thought out plot. He had been asked to hasten to the roadhouse. Naturally he would leave his home by the front door. With the light behind him he would present an easy target for the gunner. Had he been placed on the spot?

There was no time to think that over. He had reached the kitchen, a place dark and lonely. The shades were down at the windows, and it was impossible to distinguish objects in the room. This did not matter; he was not going to remain in the kitchen.

Finding the door he was seeking, he opened it and passed into a small closet. There was a window here; through it he could climb out of the house. There was little possibility that anyone would be watching this window. Once outside he would have some chance to discover what was going on. The screen was in, but there was no trouble in pushing it aside. A glance showed the rear lawn, dark and awesome as the thoughts in his mind. Thirty yards away was a dark high shadow, the outline of the hedge enclosing his estate. Beyond it ran the road.

A sound began to reach his ears, the steady running of an engine, the rumbling motor of a car parked outside the hedge. As he listened he heard the motor give a sudden roar, caught the sound of clashing gears. The car was being put into motion.

He leaped out of the window, stumbling as he hit the ground, falling to his knees. On his feet in a second, he tore around the side of the house, running for the garage. He knew what the noisy starting engine implied. Whoever it was who had tried to kill him was now fleeing. In the garage were his own cars.

The garage doors were open, and for that he was thankful. Falling into the seat of his big roadster, he fumbled with the key, then found the lock. As his foot pushed down on the gas, the engine sputtered into life. Playing with the choke for a second, he waited until the sound became a steady purr, then backed out into the drive. In a wide sweeping circle he turned toward the road.

Before reaching the opening in the hedge, he was in second; by the time he was on the road, the car was in high. The highway turned just past his house, running down a steep hill on its winding way to the city. As he reached the crest of the hill, he saw half way down its length the red tail light of a fleeing machine.

The car ahead was sliding from one side of the road to the other, hurtling down the hill at a speed much too great for a light machine. His was a powerful car, the fastest that had as yet been turned out.

That he could overtake the car ahead he knew; just what he would do when he reached its side was another problem.

With the long roadster picking up in speed every second, he started down the hill. Ahead was a fleeing car, one which no doubt held the person who had tried to kill him, a car lurching all over the road, swaying and bounding as it rushed along. Long before reaching the city limits he would be able to pass it.

The light upon the dashboard played over his speedometer. The needle was swaying over seventy, creeping to seventy-five, coming to rest on a trembling eighty. There were plenty more miles in the engine, but on the steep hill the speed he was making was sufficient.

The red tail light vanished for a moment as the road swept around a curve. Skidding around the half turn, he saw it disappearing around the second curve. When he reached this it had gone, though the road ran a straight arrow before him.

With his brakes screeching forth a shrieking protest, the car came to a skidding stop; then he noticed a road to his left. It was a dirt road, twisting a roundabout way to the city, passing over at least a dozen railroad tracks. When he turned on to its rough surface his eyes picked up again the red tail light.

He had to drive more slowly now, for the road was narrow, its surface badly rutted; but he was drawing closer every moment. Now he could make out the back of the coupe ahead, a low, squatty, vague square of blackness. He could not see through the back window, for whoever was driving had turned the dash light off.

Curving and twisting, the road ran through fields, past cheap small houses. A railroad track was bumped over, then another, to be followed by a straight piece of dirt. It was here that he saw the approaching train and at the first glimpse knew that it would be difficult to beat it to the crossing.

To his left, hurtling through the darkness, could be seen the onrushing headlight of an express. The whistle was loudly shrilling through the night, a long piercing warning of danger. Ahead was the swinging red light above the crossing.

The coupe was closer to the track by at least a hundred yards. Manners' foot went slamming down on the brake as he saw the small car give an extra burst of speed, watched it pass the swinging light and bounce roughly over the tracks. Then, as with a creaking protest the brakes gripped, he stopped ten feet from the train, which went rattling noisily over the crossing.

Though it was one of the fastest trains in the country, yet as he watched the lights of the car windows rush by he wondered if it would ever end. The delay was short, but when the last car darted by, and he threw in his clutch, he realized that the delay had been long enough to allow the car ahead to escape. As he bumped over the rails he could no longer see the red tail light ahead.

Bringing the speed of the car down to forty, he decided to go at once to the police station. To try to find the other machine would be useless. He was on the outskirts of the city, a place of small homes, with countless lanes and roads running to the main highway. Down any one of them the car could have darted to safety.

All the way to the city he was thinking wild, angry thoughts. Never again would he have such a narrow escape from death. If he had not stepped back from the door, the bullet would have struck him down. Who could have wished to kill him? So far as he knew, Manners did not have an enemy in the world. Tolerant and liberal in his thinking, he went his way through life, bothering with no one, willing to allow everyone to do as he wished. That anyone should hate him enough to try to kill him caused a sinking feeling in his heart. But someone did.

If he had not known Zuko, the telephone call and the insistence that he must come to the roadhouse would have given the answer. If any man had ever been placed on the spot for a killing, it had been himself when he opened that front door. Yet, this must have been just a coincidence.

Could it be because of the library murder? It must be; yet after all he knew nothing about the murder except what he had been told. Whoever had killed the woman and Spicer had been driven to the deed by fear. The murderer had nothing to fear from him. Could it be he thought that he had? If so what was it he thought Manners knew?

The car went running past the new million-dollar high school. Turning, he went through a small park; the park ended, he came out into the public square. In front of him the river wound its way to the lake, and across the bridge he saw the dark outlines of the police station and library. As he came to a stop he had decided that the shooting was in some unknown manner connected with the two murders.

He found Rogan alone in his office, apparently trying to read a mass of reports. One glance at his friend's face and he thrust the papers to one side. Something had excited Manners, made him angry. There was a red flush in the young man's cheeks and he was more excited than Rogan had ever seen him.

Wondering what could be the trouble, he ventured a question.

Many had been the stories told in Rogan's dingy office. Into that quiet room flowed a stream of men and women with anguish, hatred and sorrow in their hearts. Stories of the depths to which human passions could fall, sordid accounts of human hatred and passion had been poured into the ears of the whitehaired chief, but the story his friend was telling was one of the most perplexing he had heard.

When, with amazed feeling in his voice, Manners told of going to the door, and of the shot which had come flashing out of the darkness, Rogan's first thought had been that the professor was fooling. A look at the tensed, set face, the sound of the repressed feeling in the cultured voice drove the thought away. It had happened, yet it seemed impossible.

When the voice died away, Rogan reached into his desk and brought forth a well blackened pipe. Slowly the tobacco was patted into a worn bowl, more slowly was the match applied. Without looking at the professor he ventured a question.

"So you think it's mixed up with the murders?" The retort was short and vigorous. As he heard it, Rogan raised one of his eyebrows and his hand picked up a paper from the desk. A glance, and he turned in his chair to look at Manners. When he opened his lips, what he said had nothing to do with the story he had just heard. Slowly he began to tell what he had discovered about Spicer. He reminded Manners that, if the librarian had been in financial difficulties, there might be some suspicion that he had stolen the pamphlets. A detective had interviewed the banks, had looked into Spicer's safe deposit box. The librarian had not been in need of money.

He described Spicer's being called to the telephone. The men with whom he had been playing bridge had been interviewed. The game had been arranged several days before; the evening was to be spent in the club. A bellboy had come to the table a little after nine, saying that the librarian was wanted on the telephone. Upon Spicer's return to the card room, he seemed rather excited, saying that he must go out at once, though he expected to return within a hour, perhaps sooner.

"Then he was not going far," Manners commented.

Rogan nodded at the interruption, but did not say anything about it. Instead he told of the joking remarks which were made to Spicer by the three men with whom he had been playing. The jokes had made no impression, for the librarian had been disturbed and very serious. When he did not return at ten-thirty the three men had left the club for their respective homes.

There was another bit of information. Someone of the homicide squad had stumbled upon a young man who had been parked just a few yards from the entrance of the Hunt estate. A petting party, was the chief's dry comment, but the youth had observed a blue coupe drive through the iron gate. The time had been close to midnight.

"Did he see inside the car?"

Rogan threw him a long calculating look before replying, then:

"Yes, two persons were in the coupe. A man was driving, and the young man in the parked machine had a glimpse of another figure in the car."

"Spicer, dead."

The chief agreed, though his tone was thoughtful. A murderer who would drive a car over the city's streets with the body of his victim upon the seat beside him was the type of criminal he did not like.

There was a cold-heartedness about it which spoke of a man willing to take all sorts of chances, a criminal it would be difficult to catch. Resisting an inclination to comment upon this, he reached to the desk for another slip of paper. After glancing at it he frowned.

"Here is a report on that Wellman woman. I don't see just why you wanted it."

"Rogan, that woman is out of place in the library, the one person who does not seem to fit in there. Can you think of the women who work there being seen on the dance floor at Zuko's? That reminds me, she tried to get into Miss Merton's office while I was there, had a key."

"Well," with a grunt, "I guess you are right about her not being the sort you would expect in a library. She spends more money than she earns. Her husband is only a clerk in the post office, yet she drives around in a two-thousand-dollar car, steps out, and has been running around with someone. My operators did not discover who the man was, but we will. A hard-boiled baby, that girl."

Manners nodded. After all the report had revealed nothing. Yet he could not dismiss the thought that the woman was the one thing in the library which needed watching. The memory of the dance hall swept over him, again he saw her swaying figure. One thing was certain, the Bagdad was the last place in the city where a member of the library staff should be seen.

He glanced at his watch, saw that it was tentwenty. If they were to arrive at Zuko's by eleven, it was time they started. Volunteering this information, he was met by a grunt. Very slowly and deliberately the chief pulled open a drawer and brought forth a powerful looking revolver, a gun which was carefully examined before it went into the pocket of the blue coat. Then, with a half scowl, he rose from his chair to follow Manners from the room.

Past the outskirts of the city, Manners began to let his car out. The night was dark, the feeling of moisture in the air telling of an approaching storm. Wind was sweeping in from the lake, in sudden little gusts. Far away could be heard the low heavy whistle of a boat, no doubt a freighter bound up the lake.

They did not speak. Both were a little uneasy about their approaching call. Crouched down in the seat, one hand holding on to his hat, Rogan was remembering that there were many people in the world whom he liked far better than the man he soon would see. If the chief had his way, could have his hands untied for a single day, Zuko and his kind would be blasted out of existence. Not until they had turned from the main road and were running towards the house did the chief speak. With a half grunt he turned to the silent man at his side.

"Harley, Harlen was in the office this afternoon. Had two women and Harlen brought in again. Wanted to make sure they had overlooked nothing about their visit to the office the afternoon the old dame was killed." The recollection seemed far from a happy one, for he swore in a disgusted fashion.

"But, Harlen did ask me one question, and it set me thinking. He wanted to know if anyone stole that money which was on the desk."

There was a sudden sickening skid as the heavy machine went sliding to the side of the road, to be pulled back with a jerk. Thrown upright, Rogan demanded violently why Manners did not look where he was going. A demand which brought no response.

"You don't think we have been all wrong, that Joe White does know something?" the chief queried. They had reached the barred gate. The car came to a stop. Through the wire fence Manners saw a slow approaching figure. Without a word he watched the gate thrown open, allowed the silent man to throw a flashlight upon their faces. Then, as they were told by a motion of a hand to proceed, he put the car in gear. Not until they were passing into the lane running through the fields did he speak.

"No. Joe knows nothing about the murder," he said.

So odd was the short response that Rogan twisted his head to look at Manners. He was unable to see clearly, for the face was a mass of shadows, but he sensed something, the tension in the tall, upright body, a sharp, biting tartness in the voice which had replied. Sinking back in the seat the chief wondered what had come over his companion.

Their entrance into the Bagdad caused a sensation. The lookout evidently knew they were coming, for, though his eyes narrowed at the sight of the blue uniform, he threw the door open at once. As they stepped into the bar, someone gave a startled exclamation at the sight of Rogan. Glasses were hastily replaced on the long shining surface of the bar; men turned their faces to one side to escape recognition.

His lips a tight line, Rogan followed Manners through the bar into the short hall. The stern face had not glanced either to the right or to the left. He passed by the dozen men who were drinking without a look. There had been no need to look.

That one flashing glance as he came through the door, and the face of everyone in the place was stamped in his mind, faces, in some cases, of persons he knew rather well.

Zuko's voice followed the knock on the door and, with Manners in the lead, they entered the room. Rogan's eyes passed over the book-lined walls, noticed the costly rugs upon the floor, the etchings upon the wall. Then they rested on the fat little figure who was coming to their side. Not a line in Rogan's face moved as the gangster reached out a hand to tell him he was honored in having the chief in his place. Though for a second his firm grip touched the soft fat palm, he refused Zuko's plea that he might bring them a drink.

As he sank down in a chair, the chief's hand slid over his coat pocket. There was a lump in that pocket, a hard outline he was pleased to feel. Nor did the smile with which Zuko watched the motion cause the chief to feel differently. He was glad the gun was in his pocket.

Silence fell upon the room. In it the fat little man walked over to the fireplace and stood with his back against the wall. An odd looking figure, thought Manners, fat, shapeless and ungainly. Though the heavy cheeks seemed flabby and coarse, the eyes which slowly studied them were keen and sharp. A glance which did not waver, cold, calculating and shrewd, swept over them. Seeing it, a wave of resentment came over Manners, as he remembered the shot spitting out in the darkness. Rising to his feet he put a sarcastic question. In return the look he received was reproachful. Then came Zuko's low deliberate voice:

"Professor, I can throw no light upon the attempt to kill you. It grieves me, that even for a moment you should think I knew. I—"

"I went to the door directly after your telephone call. When that door was open I was a wonderful target with the light behind me. There is such a thing as putting a man on the spot."

They saw a frown creep over the fat face. The man, of whom it was said that he knew more about murder than any other person in the state, threw out his fat hands in a gesture of protest.

"I have heard of such things," was the admission, and the gesture was that of a man claiming that one could not believe everything one heard. "Have read of them. But I am assuring you, Professor, in this case it would not be true." The voice grew hard. "Was not."

There was reproach in the eyes which looked at him. With a nod Manners shifted his glance, studying an etching across the room. There, a great artist had etched a ship with all sails set. Zuko's voice brought his eyes again to the gangster's face.

"I sent for you two tonight because I think something will take place here in a few moments which might interest you both."

For a moment the keen little eyes studied them both; then the low voice went on.

"As you know, I have a few rooms on the second floor. Often I have guests, who, shall we say, are rather shy about being seen by others, guests who wish to remain in seclusion for a little while."

Rogan's lips snapped tight. He knew all about the shy guests of whom Zuko was speaking, knew also a great deal concerning the rooms on the second floor. More than once they had been used as a hiding place by those who wished to keep out of sight for a while. He would like to tell Zuko what he thought of him, but the man was speaking again.

"Often times my guests wish seclusion. That's why we have the balcony running round the rear of the place, with an outside stairway leading up from the ground, in order that those who have my rooms need not come through the bar or be seen by any who come to drink and dance."

The tone was serious, the inflection of the low voice cold and hard. As he looked at the grotesque figure leaning against the fireplace, Manners was wondering just what he was going to say. It would be important. The grave voice held no levity in its tone. Zuko would not have insisted upon their driving from the city unless he had something important to tell them.

"I never need the police to settle my own difficulties, but at eleven o'clock, in one of those rooms above, a woman will be keeping an appointment with a man. She made it this afternoon. I have seen this woman here several times. She"—he paused to look gravely at the two men before him—"she works in the public library."

Rogan was on his feet, his heavy voice breaking into an eager question. There came a wave from Zuko's hand, a little shake of his head.

"I know nothing about the woman, chief. I have my suspicions. Though the papers have not as yet tried to fasten the library murder on me," a sarcastic smile broke over the fat face, "who knows what they will say later? All I am going to do is to take you into the room next to where the woman will be. I do not know whom she is going to see, or what it is all about; but the walls are very thin, and—"

With a shrug of his shoulders he left the sentence uncompleted, to look at his watch. Moving away from the fireplace he came to a pause by the desk in the center of the room.

"You see, chief, I really would not have given you this information, only murder and libraries do not go together. I don't know what you will discover, perhaps nothing. But if you will follow me, you can be in the room before the woman arrives. It is just eleven now."

CHAPTER SEVENTEEN

The room in which they were waiting had a window, but it was so black outside that it failed to relieve the darkness which enfolded them. To see even a hand before their faces was an impossibility. The only bit of light trickled in from the hall, creeping through the narrow crack below the door. It was a small room, dark, gloomy, over whose floor they dared not walk because of the creaking boards. Zuko had led them to the second floor, bowing them into the small room, only to leave them alone. There had been just time to give one quick glance around, then, following Zuko's suggestion, they had put out the light. It was the typical room of a roadhouse, with a small table flanked by two chairs and, along the wall, a couch. It was upon the couch they were both sitting.

As he left them, Zuko had ventured the opinion that they would not have a long wait. That had been ten minutes ago, and they had heard nothing. Manners could hear the heavy breathing of the chief by his side, felt the couch sway uneasily as Rogan moved. From outside they could catch the sound of the wind, a low steady murmur which was increasing. Under the wind the surf was starting to rise and before morning would be pounding upon the shore. Just why they were waiting in the dark, Manners could not tell. A woman from the library was coming to the room on the other side of the thin board wall. Stella Wellman, no doubt. But could they trust Zuko? Trust him they must, and deep down in his heart he knew they could. Whom the woman expected to meet he could not tell, though he had a vague suspicion he might be able to name the man, a suspicion which had only commenced to form in his mind.

The darkness pressed close around him, not a pleasant blackness, but a dark deep pit which had assumed a threatening thickness. The room had vanished, to be replaced by a vast expanse of space. Time had long since departed; it seemed as though he had been hours upon that couch. If it had not been for the heavy breathing of the chief, he would have felt very lonely.

How long they sat there he was never able to decide. Seconds slipped into minutes, minutes which seemed endless. Not a sound came from the floor below. Evidently the dance hall was not open, for they were unable to hear the orchestra. The wind, however, could be heard, a sinister wind, starting to shriek and whistle around the side of the house.

Then, just as he thought he could sit still no longer, Rogan's hand clasped his arm.

Out in the hall could be heard the sound of footsteps. Sharp, tapping footsteps they were, of a woman walking rapidly down the narrow passage. As he listened he heard a door flung open, followed by a hand fumbling on the wall in the next room. Then came the sound of the door being shut, and they could hear someone moving about in the next room. This room would be similar to the one in which they were. It could be approached by coming up from the first floor or by climbing the stairs which ran outside of the building. There was a small veranda running around the second story of the roadhouse, a convenient thing, allowing those who wished security to reach the second floor without being seen.

There was only a plain rough wall between the two rooms, and the walls were thin. With his ear pressed close to the partition, Manners could hear someone walking in the next room. She was nervously pacing the floor, walking with quick, sharp taps of her heels, a nervous woman, he thought, who would be unable to sit in a chair but was walking back and forth over the floor.

Suddenly the nervous walking came to a stop. Pressed close against the wall, Manners could almost feel the woman standing in a tensed attitude, listening. There came a soft scraping sound; a window was being opened. They heard a step, heavier than the woman's, the sound of a man walking across the floor. Silence for a second, broken by the angry, protesting voice of the woman.

They could feel the anger, a cruel, cutting hatred, though the words could not be distinguished. A heavier voice started to protest, a voice kept low in tone, as the man flung some angry retort at the unseen woman, a retort which failed to stop the words spilling from the angry lips, words which were becoming distinguishable now, as the voice rose in volume.

Whatever was happening in the other room, it was no lovers' meeting. There was no softness in the raging tones of the woman, no kindness in the man's voice as he responded. Though the man was keeping his voice low, yet Manners knew that anger would soon cause it to become loud. He felt that he ought to recognize the voice; somewhere he had heard it before.

The two voices died away for a second, and the listeners heard the woman's sharp heels go tapping across the floor. Once, twice they followed her nervous footsteps, then there was a pause, and they judged she must be standing directly opposite to where they were listening. Suddenly her voice snapped out, icy in its utter contempt.

"Tried to double-cross me. I told you you would have to give me half of what you got for those pamphlets. Told you."

There came a sharp indrawn breath at Manners' side. Rogan's hand gripped his arm, the fingers sinking into his flesh. Brushing off the grip, Manners pressed his ear close to the rough board, heard the woman's foot tapping the floor.

"Thought you would get away with it," came the sneering voice. "Well, you don't. Get me, you don't. Just let me tell the police what I know, and they will ask you who croaked Ruby Merton. What would you tell them?"

There came a violent oath from the unseen man. There was a curious undertone in the expression, a tone which caused Manners to half rise from the couch. He sank back as the woman raged forth again.

"Now you are coming across. Get me? I am not going to let you get away with it. Half is mine—"

The voice gasped out to an astonished silence.

Then suddenly came a half shriek, a cry filled with terror, and wild despairing horror.

"What are you going to do? God, what—"

Like a sudden clap of thunder there came the sharp barking report of a gun. The woman's cry died away to a sobbing note, as the gun spoke again. Rogan pulled Manners to his feet. They dashed across the floor, tried to find the door, heard, as they groped along the wall, a chair overturned in the next room. Then came a silence more sinister than any sound.

Manners' hand fell on the door knob and he jerked it open. They were in a hall; at the farther end a dim light could be seen. Their hands fumbled for the knob of the door leading into the next room. It refused to open. Pulling Manners to one side, Rogan went to the opposite side of the hall, then, with a dash, went crashing against the closed door.

With a splintering, creaking noise, it fell from its hinges.

Across the threshold they stopped short for the barest part of a second. It was a small room containing the usual table, couch and two chairs. One of the chairs was on its side. They noticed that the window opening on the veranda was open. But none of these things held their gaze. There was only one object in the room which was of any importance. Sprawled out in an odd attitude on the floor, with her head lying close to the wall and one arm extended upward against the wooden boards, lay the still figure of the woman. As they looked, they saw the arm start to fall slowly to the floor, heard a deep low moan come gasping from the white lips. Then they rushed to her side.

The examination was hasty, and when Rogan rose to his feet there came a slow shake of his head. She had been shot twice and, though he managed to stop the bleeding, yet he felt certain death was close. The proud, self-willed face was white; the lips already were colorless. To move her to the city meant that she would die before reaching the hospital; to leave her without aid meant the same.

A sound by the door caused them to whirl around. Zuko was hurrying into the room, his round face flushed with the exertion and breathing heavily. Over his shoulder were the wild staring faces of two attendants, and they could hear excited voices down the hallway. The shot had alarmed the roadhouse, and its patrons were crowding to the second floor.

As Manners thought it over later, what followed was a confused mixture of noise and rushing round. They were fortunate in one thing; there was a doctor in the bar, and in a moment he was in the room.

The woman was placed on the couch and everyone sent from the room as the physician did what he could. To move her would be impossible; as to saving her life, he did not know.

Three hours later, with his mind a confused mass of tangled emotions, Manners unlocked his own front door and came into the darkened hallway. The dog had been waiting patiently on the veranda; he followed his master into the house then led the way into the kitchen. Here Manners poured himself a tall drink, and, after a glance into the glass, added an inch more of yellow liquid. If ever he needed a drink, it was now.

There had been three hours of wild confusion. Telephone calls had been made; police officers arrived in noisy motors; people had been examined; sharp questions had been answered by frightened or angry voices. And all to no avail. No one had seen the man who had escaped through the window; no one knew how he had managed to get away unobserved.

While the police were scurrying over the grounds, or talking to the people they had herded into the dance room, upstairs, in a roughly furnished room, Stella Wellman was lying at the point of death.

There had been several times when the doctor by her side thought she had slipped away. But when Manners drove from the roadhouse the girl was still alive. How long she would live was doubtful. To move her was impossible. Doctors and nurses had been summoned from the hospital; everything was being done that medical science knew. And as the doctors worked over her, seated close beside the couch was the uneasy figure of a policeman, waiting until the closed eyes should open and she could gasp out a dying declaration.

Slowly sipping his drink, Manners realized that the circle of the library murders had been completed. That there would be any more attempts at murder he doubted. What was more, a cold certainty was in his mind. He knew who had killed the helpless old woman, whose hands had fired the shot which took Spicer's life, whose voice they had heard as they listened in the dark room of the roadhouse.

He knew, but to convince Rogan would be a difficult task. There must be proof, proof so outstanding that no one in the city would ever have a doubt. The proof might be difficult to secure. There had been in a sense, no clues. What was more, there had not been a suspect. Yet all the time, sheer cold logic had been pointing in one direction.

The glass drained, Manners poured another inch of Scotch, swallowed it quickly, then he hastened into his living room. Though it was very late, there was important work to be done. Turning on the wall lights, he bent down before one of the bookcases, searching for two books he knew were there. Both were found without difficulty.

At the desk he found some paper. Seating himself in the big chair, he turned page after page of the thin book, wrote address after address. When the end of the book was reached, he reread what had been written upon three pages of paper, then nodded. The list was correct. Rising to his feet he went over to another bookcase, here he found the directory he wished.

It was a sleepy Western Union operator who answered his telephone call. He gave his name, then told her he would give a long list of addresses to which the same telegram was to be sent. The process took a long time, but when it was over, the largest cities in America had been named. The telegram was a long one. First, he wished to know if any of the book dealers had bought, within the past few months, the Mounts Relation or the Davenport pamphlet. If so, would they describe the seller, and answer at once.

There was a second telegram which went to a small Western city. He had carefully worded the message, for the information he was seeking might not exist. But when the operator repeated it he was rather certain it would bring the result he was after.

Back again in the living room, he found a largescale map of the city and spread it flat upon his desk. There was only one section of interest, the lines which showed the unsettled territory around the Hunt estate. For many minutes he bent over the map, his long fingers tracing many roads, looking for the little squares which designated the houses.

When he had found what he was seeking, a city directory joined the map on the table.

Satisfied in the end, he leaned back in his chair to light his pipe. Whoever had murdered Spicer had not killed him at the place where the body was found. The crime had been committed elsewhere, the murderer driving to the sunken garden with the body of his victim beside him on the seat. Of one thing Manners felt sure.

It took cold nerve to drive over a road with a dead man seated beside one, more courage if the man had died by your hand. It did not stand to reason that the

murderer could live very far from the place Spicer had
been found. Cool and unemotional as the murderer might
be, after all the ride would have to be a short one.
Manners had looked for a name, the name of one living
fairly near the estate, and had found it.

Half asleep he let the pipe go out, for a while allowing
his mind to wander. From the theft of the pamphlets to
the shooting of Stella Wellman, events had moved
rapidly. But there was no rhyme or reason to all the
violence. The first murder might have been logical; the
shooting of Spicer and the girl was not. The brain behind
the crimes must be one which had emotionally gone to
pieces, the brain of an individual who was so selfcentered, so crazed with fear, that no crime, no matter
how horrible, would frighten him—a repressed neurotic,
one with a shrewd, skilled coolness, who cared not what
he did.

It was almost four when Manners climbed into bed.
No matter what happened in the morning, he intended to
stay in bed until noon. Just as he drifted off to sleep there
came a shudder. He could see again the spit of flame upon
his lawn, hear the picture go crashing to the floor. Why
anyone should try to kill him was now clear. The
murderer of Ruby Merton had become a crazed
individual, suspicious of everyone who had been engaged
in the case. With this thought in his mind he went to
sleep. It was long after noon when he came into the
dining room for the meal that was to be a combination of
lunch and breakfast. He had given a hasty look at the
table in the hall, but as yet there had been no answers to
his telegrams. But the morning paper lying beside his
plate gave him all the response which he needed. The
first page contained heavy black headlines.

If the Star had been incensed at the police before,
now they were roused to a bitter, wild anger. In short,
sharp sentences they told of the murder of Spicer.
Manners' face grew grave as he read the word "murder."
Though the news story revealed that the police had no

more information than on the previous night, the death of
Spicer had aroused a hysterical hatred in the heart of the
editor of the Star.

"Two members of the library staff have been
murdered," was the first sentence of the editorial, "and
the police have done nothing."

Who would be the next victim, who upon the library
staff was safe from a violent death? In biting, sarcastic
lines, the paper offered a reward of five thousand dollars
for any information which would lead to the arrest of the
murderer. Then it said, coldly and bitterly, that the time
had come for a shake-up on the police force.

From the chief down, the officials must go. With a
little shake of the head, Manners looked for the account
of the shooting at the Bagdad. He found it on the second
page, a short item saying that a woman had been
attacked in the roadhouse and was now lying unconscious
and at the point of death in the hospital. As for details,
the name of the woman, the circumstances of the
shooting, there were none. Either the story had come in
too late for the morning edition or else Rogan had not
given out the facts.

As he placed the paper aside, he decided that the
latter was the explanation. The story of the shooting of
Stella Wellman would have aroused the city to an excited
frenzy, if all the facts were known. Rogan had been wise
in keeping back the details. The woman was still
unconscious, the paper said, so the police were without
any information as to her assailant. Three crimes, two
deaths, and no clues. The first telegram arrived just as he
finished his lunch, and from then on they kept arriving
all afternoon. It was almost six before he received the
message he was expecting. It came from one of the best
known firms of book dealers of the country, a long
telegram saying that two weeks ago they had bought two
copies of the Mounts Relation and a copy of the
Davenport Report. They mentioned that they had paid
ten thousand dollars for the pamphlets and gave a

description of the man from whom they had been purchased.

As a description it could have been far more complete, but when the telegram was carefully placed in his pocket, Manners knew that he needed but one more message. His theory was falling into place.

There were still wide gaps to be filled, incidents which could not be explained, but as he ate his early dinner he was confident that he alone had any suspicion as to who had committed the murders.

The last telegram came at the moment when his grandfather clock was striking seven. As he tore off the edge of the envelope he hesitated a second before pulling out the flimsy yellow sheet of paper. One glance at the faint letters and his lips went shut. Now he was positive.

As he started to drive down toward the city, cresting the hill to begin the long descent, Manners' eyes were glued upon the road ahead. By lifting his head he could have glimpsed the lighted streets, long lines of flame in the darkness, but he did not look; with his eyes glued to the road he was thinking.

Once before he had been fated to be the one who unraveled a sinister crime. It had been done by a trick, though his reasoning had been correct. Once in a while his conscience reminded him of the trick he had played, and there were times when he wondered if he had acted decently. Now a similar problem confronted him.

Who had committed the murders he alone could say. The conclusion had not been brought about by the skillful picking up of clues, the weaving of a network of evidence. Clues were almost nonexistent. It was true that when news of the stealing of the pamphlets circulated among the dealers in rare books, they would become suspicious. The man who had purchased them would remember, and from that it might be possible to trace the murderer, but this he doubted. Unless there was more evidence than he had, .the individual would escape.

Should he trick him into a confession? He pondered over this as he drove toward the city. Then, as he started to skirt a long row of dingy tenement houses, he made up his mind. The murders had been vicious, useless things, the killing of individuals who were of value to the community—useless, because they were unnecessary; vicious, because the murderer was whipped into a wild frenzy of fear and, without a doubt, was emotionally irresponsible. It was his duty to unmask the criminal.

At the police station he found Rogan sitting in his office. The low room was filled with villainous smoke from the bowl of a pipe which should have been destroyed months before. The chief had taken off his coat, and in his shirt sleeves was engaged in writing a report. Evidently it was an important document, for the big hand was pausing after each word. At the sound of the opening door, he whirled around to give a quick look across the floor.

There had been a scowl upon Rogan's face, but as he watched Manners cross the floor to stand by his desk he motioned to a chair. With a shake of his head the professor refused the invitation. For a second he stood glancing down at the chief. It was a weary man he saw. The red face was in sad need of a shave; dark circles were around the baggy eyes; the white hair was rumpled. Manners could see that the police head was in bad humor. For a moment he looked, then asked a question:

"How about Stella Wellman?"

There came a slow shake of the white head, as an uneasy expression flitted over the round face. "We got her down to the hospital this morning.

So far she has been unable to talk; in fact, she is still unconscious. They operated on her about three, and she may not come through. If she could only talk for a moment!"

There came a long sigh from the chief's lips. As he heard it, Manners bent across the desk, his voice low and serious.

"Rogan, you realize of course that we are not dealing with any normal murderer. You know that the person must be someone crazed with fear, whipped up to a killing frenzy also, I think, by drugs. And all along we have made one mistake."

The seriousness of the tone caused the big chair to be pushed back. From under his shaggy eyebrows Rogan looked at his friend. What he saw upon Manners' face caused him to sit upright. He hurled a question across the desk.

"What mistake?"

"We have been trying all along to figure out how the murderer could get into Ruby Merton's office without being seen. We decided she must have unlocked the door leading into the hall to let someone in. Suppose she did not. Suppose someone who was in that office during the afternoon took the key from the door. When he returned through the hallway he unlocked the door with the stolen key. Suppose that is what happened? Of course no one would see him."

Rogan started to speak, but Manners had left the desk and was walking across the floor. With a hand upon the door he paused.

"I am going to run up and have a little talk with Harlen about his visit to the office," he said. Then, without another word, he left the room.

As the door closed, Rogan made a half attempt to rise, only to sink back in his seat. For a while he sat silent, his face grave, his brow knit. Manners had been gone but twenty minutes when, with a sudden start, the chief leaped to his feet. For an instant he stood as if unable to credit the idea which had swept into his mind. Then with a sudden vicious oath he sprang into action.

He jerked on his coat, found his hat, and started for the door, but turned when half way across the floor to dart back to his desk, yank open a drawer, and thrust a gun into his pocket. He dashed out of the room, ran down the hallway, and paused before a door marked "private."

With a jerk he opened the door and looked into a room filled with his men.

As he came through the door he was barking out commands, which all ended with the same word, "Hurry!"

CHAPTER EIGHTEEN

Outside the city limits Harley Manners brought his car to a stop, as he gloomily studied a dark unkempt field to his right. It sloped away from the street and, at the lower edge, he could glimpse a low one-story cottage. The field should have been a closely cropped lawn, but it was a neglected underbush of tall weeds. The trees, which cast somber shadows over the high grass, were old and sadly in need of trimming.

Nothing of what he saw appealed to him, nor was he feeling very cheerful over the coming interview. There were persons in the city who loudly said that the man he was going to see was crazy. Manners knew Harlen was odd and would resent his call. Anyway, there was just one question he wished to ask him, though he did wonder what the answer might be.

In a sense Professor Harlen was a public character, if being a public character means to be well-known in a city's life. He possessed a keen, brilliant mind, yet again and again there had been occasions when his ungovernable temper and biting sarcasm had caused him trouble. There were many who admired his intellect, though those who really liked him were few.

With a shrug of his shoulders as he thought that the coming interview would prove far from agreeable, Manners turned off the gas and stepped from the machine. Harlen might receive him pleasantly; then again, he might slam the door in his face. Be that as it may, he intended to ask the question which had caused him to ride up the hill from the police station.

As he walked up the winding path, he wondered why the grounds had been allowed to fall into such decay. The grass was high, evidently not having been cut all summer, with weeds everywhere. The little house he was approaching had not been painted in some years; the railing around the porch was in sad need of repairing; yet Harlen himself was known for the carefulness with which he wore his clothes.

Odd that he should have allowed his house and grounds to fall into such a condition.

Approaching the cottage, Manners saw the faint glimmer of a light shining through a side window. The man was evidently in, and he climbed the steps and pounded on the door. There came a long wait, another knock, then a third. Above his head the trees were creaking in the wind, but save for that it was silent. From within the house came no sound.

Manners knew there was a light within, so for the fourth time his hand pounded against the door. Someone must be in, and no doubt could hear his knock. For the fifth time his hand went banging against the unresponsive door. Just on the verge of deciding that he might as well go back, he heard a faint sound from the hall. Not only did he hear a sound but he became conscious that someone was looking at him, could feel eyes searching over his figure. High in the door he saw a little slot. Though he could see nothing else, yet he knew that he was being examined.

There came the sound of someone fumbling with the door knob, then, very deliberately, the door was pushed open. Standing in the doorway, with the light from the hall playing over his thin figure, stood the well-dressed professor. His face was expressionless, but the questioning eyes startled Manners, cold, dilated, angry eyes, burning with a repressed rage and hatred.

"Professor Harlen," Manners began, as the cold glance swept over him, "I came up from the chief of police because he wished me to ask you a question."

"I have told the chief all I know," was the icy retort as the door began to close. Then the motion suddenly paused, as though the man within had changed his mind. It opened again and the thin figure stood close to the wall. He made a motion with his hand, a motion to enter.

Manners looked down a long hallway, noticed the doors leading to unseen rooms. Stepping over the threshold, he heard the door slammed shut behind him, heard a more curious sound, the key being turned in its lock. Then, still without a word, the man brushed by him and, opening a door, stood to one side to allow Manners to enter the room.

It was not a large room, and it was far from being in order. There were bookcases around three walls, even books piled upon the floor. Under a bright electric light was a table, its surface littered with pamphlets. It seemed evident that the place had not been dusted for years.

Motioning Manners to a chair, Harlen walked over to the table to pick up a half smoked cigar. As he relighted it; his gloomy eyes kept boring over to the chair where Manners had seated himself.

It was not a pleasant look; behind the dark eyes struggled rage, mingled with a trace of wonder.

As he saw the look, observed the uneasy twitching of the man's lips, the nervous trembling of the thin body, Manners decided that Harlen was close to the breaking point.

"Well," came the cold voice. "You wanted to ask me a question. Go ahead."

Instead of speaking, Manners allowed his glance to sweep the room. Past the bookcases his eyes traveled, coming to rest upon an open door. Through it he could look into the dim interior of a bedroom. What he saw caused his eyes suddenly to narrow.

Upon the floor, close to the door, lay two suitcases with covers thrown back, their interiors half filled with clothes. Harlen must have been interrupted in packing when Manners pounded upon the door. In the uneasy silence there came the harsh rasping voice:

"What did you wish to ask me?"

"You told the chief yesterday—or rather, asked him about the money which was lying on the desk in Miss Merton's office."

"Well, suppose I did?" was the answer. Though the expression upon the sullen twitching face did not change, Manners felt the wild intensity of the piercing glance, noticed the trembling hands, which were being slowly closed into fists.

"I wondered about your question," he said slowly, with his eyes on the man's face, "wondered how you knew there was any money on her desk. You were in there around three-thirty; the money was not on her desk until about five. How did you happen to know that it was there? You must have returned to the office. Why?"

A startled, frightened surprise swept over the dark face. Then came an unexpected action. Instead of replying, Harlen rushed across the floor and threw open the door leading to the hall, stepping to one side as he did so. Manners needed no words to explain the gesture. He was being asked to leave the house. Rising to comply with the unspoken request, he was moved by an unexplained impulse to look at the wall directly across from his chair.

His eyes, passing over the heap of magazines and pamphlets upon the desk, saw a couch at the side of the room and above it a fish net draped upon the wall. It was a faded fish net, made from black cord. The cord was similar to that which had been found around Ruby Merton's throat.

His hands gripping the arms of the chair for support, he stared blankly at the net. Just a mass of string, but black cord, similar to the one which had caused Miss Merton's death. He knew his face had grown white as he realized the significance of what he saw. Harlen had mentioned the money lying on the desk. That one question had given him away. To know about the money he had had to return to that office. Manners realized that when he turned his eyes from the net it would still be there, mute evidence against a murderer.

A sound of hurried feet, running and stumbling over the floor, caused him to look around. Harlen was by the desk, his nervous trembling hands fumbling for a drawer. With a leap Manners sprang to his feet. There was but one desire in his heart, to get out of the house, reach the safety of his parked car. Three steps were taken when he came to a sudden stop at the sound of Harlen's voice:

"I don't want to shoot you in the back."

Whirling, he saw a sardonic smile playing over Harlen's face. Then he noticed the gun in his hand, a gun whose aim did not waver, which was pointing towards his heart. Though there was still the impulse to flee, the look in the enraged and flaming eyes showed that it would be useless. An angry, waving motion of Harlen's arm motioned him back to the chair.

As he reseated himself, he knew that he was facing a man who for a moment was unbalanced. It was his suspicion that this condition was caused by a drug. The dilated eyes, the nervous trembling of the body, the face working in anger, one fist clenched tight, all spoke of drugs. Any attempt to rise and grapple with Harlen was beyond question. One step, and the gun would speak. The only thing to do was to sit still.

"So the bright professor of psychology has just discovered that I killed Ruby Merton," came the sneering voice. "What a bright professor!"

Though the voice was not raised, yet there was a curious vibrating undercurrent of hatred in the words. Anger was there, with a vicious love of cruelty, mingled with deep contempt for the man in the chair. Soon there would come an emotional out-burst. Manners hoped it would take the form of speech instead of action. At this instant the expected outburst came. In a voice rising with every word, and losing its cold, unemotional tone, the hatred and venom of months was shrilled out into the little room.

It was far from a coherent outburst. There were phrases in which, in a shrill, trembling shriek, Harlen poured out his bitter hatred of certain people. The sentences were unconnected; the phrases broken, wild, phrases which tangled together, in an odd mixture of words, the names of Spicer and Stella Wellman, words raging with egoistical contempt for the police, filled with bitter hatred for Manners. As the shrill voice went echoing through the room, Manners knew that for the time being the man's mind was unbalanced.

Sitting upright, with his eyes never leaving Harlen's face, he was hoping that the hand holding the gun would waver for a moment, that, in his wild hatred against others, Harlen would forget himself.

Though at times the eyes did turn away, the hand which held the gun kept always pointing at Manners' heart. If he made one move, the man would fire.

There came a moment when Harlen paused, more because he was out of breath than from lack of words. In the silence which fell, Manners tried to figure out how long he had listened. Though he knew it was but a few minutes, yet it had seemed hours. Then, suddenly, the shrill voice burst forth again, ringing with anger, vibrating with passion. "Think of that library hoarding pamphlets worth thousands of dollars, hoarding them to sell some day to wealthy men."

The shrill voice resounded through the room. So flushed was the thin face becoming that for a moment Manners wondered if he would burst a blood vessel. The dilated eyes were flashing, the thin figure trembling with nervousness. His own face white, Manners stared at the raging man. Before the desk stood a sinister, threatening figure of evil. Fear, whipped into a frenzy by drugs, had caused all reason to depart from the inflamed brain. Suddenly the tone changed—now it was low, sly, cunning, the voice of one who gave a little chuckle of evil.

"You are a psychologist. You must know all about women," was the sly insinuation. "Take my advice; never trust them; they are all alike. All will coax you to gain what they wish, then they will throw you aside, start to threaten and demand. But I took care of her when she threatened me."

Again the tone changed. Now it was cold, yet the lack of emotion made it more horrible thanbefore. The voice was that of one who had a purpose in his mind, a mind filled with memories which were not pleasant.

"A month ago I took those pamphlets, and then that silly old woman at the library discovered they were gone. She called me on the telephone, taunted me with exposure, threatened me, me, who have the best mind in the city. But I fixed her forever. I knew from her voice when she called me that she had discovered the substitution. So when I went to the library I took a piece of cord from the net. She tried to make me promise to return the pamphlets. I said I would. Of course I had sold them. So I took the key from the hall door and when I returned—"

He paused, throwing back his head to give a loud hysterical laugh. "She thought I was returning the books. It was easy to kill her. She had no strength."

The voice died to a whisper as a thoughtful look swept the nervous face. Harlen appeared to be thinking and he gave Manners a long, calculating look, as if trying to decide a disputed question. Crossing the floor he halted only a foot away from his victim. There was an evil, vicious grin on the face which looked down at the chair. His words were slow, cold, with an icy deliberation:

"Yes, I killed her, Manners, killed Spicer also.I had to kill him, for he would have discovered that I took the pamphlets. I called him on the telephone, got him to come out here on the statement that I knew who had killed his librarian. Once started on this sort of thing, you have to keep going. You don't like what I say," was the sneer. "Well, it won't make any difference to you. If you had not come round, I would have been off tonight. I don't care what you know. It makes no difference. You die in a moment anyway. I won't miss as I did last night."

At the last words Manners made an instinctive movement to rise. A hand thrust him roughly back into the chair as, with a snarl of rage, Harlen thrust the gun against his chest. Closing his eyes Manners wondered if he would hear the report when the gun was fired. He kept his eyes closed until a faint sound made them open.

It was a scraping sound coming from the direction of the window, an odd sound, a mixture of a faint blow and a little shove. He opened his eyes in time to see Harlen throw a suspicious glance across the room. For a second the gun in the hand wavered. As he saw this, Manners threw himself forward, his hands clutching around the professor's legs in the tackle that a football coach had once spent long weary hours drilling into him. The action was unexpected, the movement so sudden that it caught the man off guard. With a crash he fell to the floor, and as he fell the gun went spinning from his hand.

Though Manners had plenty of strength, yet as they rolled over the floor, he realized that in a rough and tumble fight he would come out second best. There was wild, frenzied fury in the hands that gripped his throat, unexpected strength in the arms that clutched him. Try his best, he was barely able to struggle out of the clutching fingers.

Over the floor he rolled, escaping for a second the reaching fingers. Then a hand fell on his shoulder and pulled him back toward the chair. As he rolled over, his eye fell upon the gun. It lay only a few inches from his fingers, a black, object against the red rug. If he could only reach it before Harlen saw it, then there would be a chance, but as his hand reached forth, the professor suddenly shook himself loose and leaped for the gun.

The long fingers clutching for the revolver almost reached it but that moment Manners' hands again clasped the long legs and brought the man with a crash to the floor. Over and over they rolled until a hand gripped Manners' throat, a hand whose pressure steadily increased, and whose sharp finger nails were cutting into his flesh. With a sudden burst of energy he threw the clasping fingers aside only to see Harlen's arm reach forth and clasp the gun.

Struggling to his feet, Manners stood swaying back and forth. There was a momentary sight of Harlen's distorted face, the enraged face of an animal, working and twisting in vicious rage. At the sight Manners sprang forward, and as he jumped he heard the sound of breaking glass and felt a rush of cool air over his face. Then came a heavy blow against his head. For an instant he seemed to hear the sound of rushing water, felt a deep darkness rising to enfold him and he sank down into a bottomless abyss. After that, he knew no more.

CHAPTER NINETEEN

The bright warm sunlight of early afternoon was playing over Harley Manners' garden. It passed through the leaves of the tall trees, danced across beds of colorful flowers, came to rest upon the wide veranda which ran around the long house, and warmed the burly person of the Chief of Police, Timothy Rogan, who was seated, very much at his ease, upon the veranda.

It was Rogan wearing a very well fitting uniform, with brass buttons glittering like gold. The round red face was fixed in a contented grin, as, leaning far back in his chair, the chief regarded the glass which he held in his hand, a tall thin glass which had just been refilled and would perhaps be refilled again. He should have been recalling what the papers had said that morning. It had been many years since any chief of police had received the flattery and praise which had been poured forth upon his head that day. "A skilled and courageous official," had been one line. "One who has solved the most difficult series of crime we have had," said another. If he was recalling them, which as it happened, he was not, he would have blushed. Rogan knew that the words of praise should have been directed to the tall, lanky young man sitting close to the veranda rail.

It was a rather languid and weary professor of abnormal psychology who sat sprawled out in the wicker chair. His gray flannel suit fitted well; his blue tie held a rare stone for the world to see; but there was a bandage around his head and his face was a little white. The effects of the previous night had not as yet worn away.

They had been sitting in the wicker chairs for many minutes. When the chief arrived at two, Manners decided he wished to be out of doors. It was peaceful and quiet upon the veranda, and the sight of the green lawn and tall trees brought rest to his soul. And rest was something he desired. Nor did they talk for a while, though there were many questions both wished to ask.

Taking a long drink from his glass, Rogan eyed the pinch backed bottle for a moment, then reached out his hand to pour an inch of yellow liquid into his glass, followed by a dash of soda. As he whirled the mixture around in the glass, he turned to his friend.

"Harley," he said in a wondering voice, "just how did you happen to spot Harlen as the man we wanted?"

There was a chuckle from the wicker chair.

"I never spotted him until you told me he was the man," was the amused comment. The glass went down upon the stand. Turning a surprised face toward the man opposite him, Rogan raised his eyebrows as though he thought the blow on the head had suddenly affected Manners' mind.

"I told you! Don't be a fool, Harley."

"You did. In fact, Harlen told you he was the person we were looking for. Remember his question about the money on Ruby Merton's table ? She placed the money there herself, a fund which had been collected by the Women's Club for a picture in a branch library. She brought that money to her office only a short while before she was murdered. No one else went in there after that, except Joe White, and she wasn't in the office then. If Harlen knew about the money, he must have been in the office again. No one knew anything about it, you never told the papers. If he knew, why then he must have seen it and might be the murderer. That slip of his made me see how the murderer got into the place. We went on the theory that she opened the door and invited him in, but I was all wrong; my psychology was not working."

"What was that you said was not working?" Rogan queried.

"Psychology. We should have remembered that if she had invited the person who had stolen the pamphlets to come to the office, she never would have opened the door for him. Why, that woman, filled with years of self-righteousness, would not have risen from her seat to open the door for a person she thought guilty of theft. We were wrong. Some one of the persons in the room during the afternoon took the key to the hall door when her attention was engaged. Now the two girls would not do that; the book salesman was barred; Joe White didn't; only Harlen was left."

He paused as a reflective look swept over his face. Again he could see the rage-swept face of the professor, hear once more the shrill, frenzied voice. He gave a little shudder as he continued:

"Now that seemed reasonable. Though at first it appeared incredible that Harlen would kill the woman and then murder Spicer, there was no one else to suspect. The trouble was that I knew little about Harlen, though I did realize that he was excitable, prone to become angry in arguments, filled with what we call a 'superiority complex.' When I came back from the Bagdad, I sent telegrams to the leading book sellers, asking if they had bought copies of the pamphlets, and begging for a description of the person from whom they had bought them. Klein of Chicago telegraphed a fair description of Harlen."

"But heavens, Harley, those little bits of paper should not have made a man commit murder."

"They caused two murders, Rogan," was the dry comment. "I wired to the University in which he once taught asking for information. The reason he lost his position was because he was at one time confined in the state insane asylum. He lost his temper at the University, assaulted a student and was dismissed. Later they found out about a breakdown he once had, discovered he had spent six months in an asylum, discovered also that he took drugs, cocaine."

"It was a crazy series of crimes," Rogan commented.

Manners nodded, going on to explain to the chief, who did not actually understand just what he had said. He told of the border line between actual insanity and the mental state of those individuals, who, though technically not insane, at times approach such a condition, in their emotional upsets. He added that there was little doubt that Harlen had fallen in love with the Wellman woman and had stolen the pamphlets either at her suggestion or with her aid. He admitted that he did not know all the actual events in each tragedy, though he judged it was violent fear of exposure which had caused the first murder. After that the man went to pieces.

"You had, I think," he said, thoughtfully, "a man whose emotions were naturally very unstable and who was using cocaine. That drug, you know destroys all moral sense. Whipped into rage by the discovery that the librarian knew of his theft of the pamphlets, he killed her. No doubt he knew the library well. Probably he had secretly met the Wellman woman there. Realizing that he had left the cord on the desk, he came back for it, and again that night, returning out of curiosity, found Rand at the safe and tried to kill him. He would be whipping up his courage with increased use of cocaine. The more he used, the greater the fear in his mind and the greater the desire to remove those in his way. This explains the useless killing of Spicer, and the attempt to shoot me, for of course he was the man on my lawn."

"The woman talked a little this morning," was Rogan's comment as he reached for the glass. He smiled at the recollection, bending forward in his chair.

"She is not going to die, though when she asked us that question this morning, we sort of hinted her stay in this world would be brief. She talked. God knows, I never was able to understand why the Lord ever makes her kind of a woman, but there are lots of them."

An expression of disgust swept over the red face as he hastily drained his glass. Manners broke in with a question. Let the chief start in with his viewpoint of the modern woman, and Manners would never know what had been said in the hospital. What Rogan told him was just about what he would have guessed she would say.

The woman, frightened by the thought of death, had admitted that she had been playing around with the professor. At first the fact that he was well known in the city had pleased her vanity. Then she discovered that he would do as she wished, and from then on she began to use him to gain what she wanted. She had told him of the rare pamphlets, had pointed out that, as no one ever looked at them, it would be easy to replace them with reprints, with little chance of the substitution being discovered for a long time. One day she had taken the first one from the safe.

How she had managed to persuade Ruby Merton to allow Harlen to borrow the two which were left, Rogan did not know. But she had succeeded, and six weeks before the murder they had been replaced in the safe, with copies substituted for the originals. On the morning of the murder she had seen the librarian looking at the pamphlets, knew from the excited horror on her face that she had discovered what had been done. As Harlen was the last one to have them in his possession, she knew at once that he would be suspected.

"She must have known that he killed her," was Manners' comment.

"Don't see how she could help it. It was after the murder she started to demand he give her half of the money he had received from their sale. That's why she went to the roadhouse. He had agreed to meet her there."

In the silence which fell, Manners was picturing the frenzied professor. He had committed one murder, only to discover that he was entangled with a woman he could not trust. Spicer had been put out of the way because

Harlen felt sure that the librarian would sooner or later discover what had happened.

He had tried to kill the Wellman woman perhaps with the hope that if she were dead he would no longer have anything to be frightened over. The whole affair was the nightmare of an unbalanced brain.

"Rogan, I suppose the girl will recover?"

"Yes," was the answer. "She will recover, and when she does, we are going to stand her up in the courtroom and send her over for a few years."

So threatening was the scowl upon the chief's face that for fear he might plunge into a discussion of his ideas as to what should be done with certain kinds of women, Manners hastily asked a question:

"How did you happen to reach Harlen's home in time to stop him from killing me?"

"When you shot off your mouth about us being wrong on that old dame letting her murderer into her office, it got me thinking and I rushed some of the boys up there. We got there just in time at that. Smashed the window at the very moment he banged you on the head."

He sighed. After all, he was getting old, and a good deal of crime had played around his career. If he had been one moment later at that window, his friend would have been the third victim.

"You know, Harley, it took three of us to cart him off. He was raving like a bug when he had the cuffs put on him. Took two of us to do it, and I have an idea he never will stand trial. You may not think he is crazy, but he sure looked like it to me when he went off in the wagon."

Tenderly Manners touched the white bandage around his head. The bruise still ached a little and there was a tight sensation around his temples. Rogan had reached the house in time to save him. He would agree with the chief's last remark. He too, doubted if Harlen would ever stand trial. Before the murders, he had been a neurotic, easily unbalanced. The strain of the fear and dread of the last few days might have caused his mind to break. But there was still another question he wished answered.

"Did you find anything in the house?"

"We did," came the reply in a triumphant tone, "Spicer's top coat. Found also a piece had been cut out of that fish net, and it's just the length and of the same material as the cord found around the old dame's neck. Found bloodstains on the rug. No doubt in my mind now that Harlen had Spicer come to the house, killed him, then drove his car to the place we found it. Have a good case even if he had not talked to you."

Manners nodded, leaning far back in his chair. Rogan went on, his voice slow, reflective:

"You know, Harley, the papers changed their tune this morning. Everything is all right down at the station now. But—"

There came a shrug of the stout shoulders. The gray eyes went down to the stand, glimpsed the pinch backed bottle. He had drunk enough, but then one more would do no harm. It was time to celebrate; the dread and the horror of the last few days had departed. His hand reached out to pick up the bottle and he smiled a little as the Scotch fell into the glass, to be thinned a moment later by the soda. For a moment he eyed the yellow liquid, giving it a slow twirl with his wrist. Then he turned to glance at his friend.

Manners' head was resting on the back of the chair, his eyes were closed, the intelligent face was peaceful. A little smile passed over Rogan's lips at the sight. He liked this young man. What could he have done without him? It seemed too bad to speak, but speak he must, and at the sound of his voice Manners' eyes opened to look smilingly over to the other chair.

"You know, Harley—now it's all over—I have come to one conclusion. We said that all the usual motives for crime would not apply in this case— revenge, money, sex—remember we said all those things."

"We did say all that. And in the end we discovered that every single one of the three was in the case. The three usual motives in murder were all there."

The white head nodded as Rogan slowly raised his glass to take a long sip. He was thinking, running over the last few days, thinking that he hoped it would be a long time before he had to face a similar situation. It was this thought which caused him to place his glass hastily on the stand and turn to his friend.

"Harley?" came his rough voice.

"Yes," replied the professor.

"Harley, never again do I want to run into Murder in a Library."

THE END

MYSTERIES BY ANNE AUSTIN

Murder at Bridge

When an afternoon bridge party attended by some of
Hamilton's leading citizens ends with the hostess being
murdered in her boudoir, Special Investigator Dundee of
the District Attorney's office is called in. But one of the
attendees is guilty? There are plenty of suspects: the
victim's former lover, her current suitor, the retired judge
who is being blackmailed, the victim's maid who had been
horribly disfigured accidentally by the murdered woman,
or any of the women who's husbands had flirted with the
victim. Or was she murdered by an outsider whose
motive had nothing to do with the town of Hamilton.
Find the answer in . . . **Murder at Bridge**

One Drop of Blood

When Dr. Koenig, head of Mayfield Sanitarium is
murdered, the District Attorney's Special Investigator,
"Bonnie" Dundee must go undercover to find the killer.
Were any of the inmates of the asylum insane enough to
have committed the crime? Or, was it one of the staff,
motivated by jealousy? And what was is the secret in the
murdered man's past. Find the answer in . . . **One Drop
of Blood**

AVAILABLE FROM RESURRECTED PRESS!

GEMS OF MYSTERY
LOST JEWELS FROM A MORE
ELEGANT AGE

Three wonderful tales of mystery from some of the best known writers of the period before the First World War -

A foggy London night, a Russian princess who steals jewels, a corpse; a mysterious murder, an opera singer, and stolen pearls; two young people who crash a masked ball only to find themselves caught up in a daring theft of jewels; these are the subjects of this collection of entertaining tales of love, jewels, and mystery. This collection includes:

- **In the Fog - by Richard Harding Davis's**

- **The Affair at the Hotel Semiramis - by A.E.W. Mason**

- **Hearts and Masks - Harold MacGrath**

AVAILABLE FROM RESURRECTED PRESS!

THE EDWARDIAN DETECTIVES
LITERARY SLEUTHS OF THE EDWARDIAN ERA

The exploits of the great Victorian Detectives, Poe's C. Auguste Dupin, Gaboriau's Lecoq, and most famously, Arthur Conan Doyle's Sherlock Holmes, are well known. But what of those fictional detectives that came after, those of the Edwardian Age? The period between the death of Queen Victoria and the First World War had been called the Golden Age of the detective short story, but how familiar is the modern reader with the sleuths of this era? And such an extraordinary group they were, including in their numbers an unassuming English priest, a blind man, a master of disguises, a lecturer in medical jurisprudence, a noble woman working for Scotland Yard, and a savant so brilliant he was known as "The Thinking Machine."

To introduce readers to these detectives, Resurrected Press has assembled a collection of stories featuring these and other remarkable sleuths in The Edwardian Detectives.

- The Case of Laker, Absconded by Arthur Morrison
- The Fenchurch Street Mystery by Baroness Orczy
- The Crime of the French Café by Nick Carter
- The Man with Nailed Shoes by R Austin Freeman
- The Blue Cross by G. K. Chesterton
- The Case of the Pocket Diary Found in the Snow by Augusta Groner
- The Ninescore Mystery by Baroness Orczy
- The Riddle of the Ninth Finger by Thomas W. Hanshew
- The Knight's Cross Signal Problem by Ernest Bramah

- The Problem of Cell 13 by Jacques Futrelle
- The Conundrum of the Golf Links by Percy James Brebner
- The Silkworms of Florence by Clifford Ashdown
- The Gateway of the Monster by William Hope Hodgson
- The Affair at the Semiramis Hotel by A. E. W. Mason
- The Affair of the Avalanche Bicycle & Tyre Co., LTD by Arthur Morrison

RESURRECTED PRESS CLASSIC MYSTERY CATALOGUE

Journeys into Mystery
Travel and Mystery in a More Elegant Time

The Edwardian Detectives
Literary Sleuths of the Edwardian Era

Gems of Mystery
Lost Jewels from a More Elegant Age

E. C. Bentley
Trent's Last Case: The Woman in Black

Ernest Bramah
Max Carrados Resurrected:
The Detective Stories of Max Carrados

Agatha Christie
The Secret Adversary
The Mysterious Affair at Styles

Octavus Roy Cohen
Midnight

Freeman Wills Croft
The Ponson Case
The Pit Prop Syndicate

J. S. Fletcher
The Herapath Property
The Rayner-Slade Amalgamation
The Chestermarke Instinct
The Paradise Mystery
Dead Men's Money

Fergus Hume
The Mystery of a Hansom Cab
The Green Mummy
The Silent House
The Secret Passage

Edgar Jepson
The Loudwater Mystery

A. E. W. Mason
At the Villa Rose

A. A. Milne
The Red House Mystery
Baroness Emma Orczy
The Old Man in the Corner

Edgar Allan Poe
The Detective Stories of Edgar Allan Poe

Arthur J. Rees
The Hampstead Mystery
The Shrieking Pit
The Hand In The Dark
The Moon Rock
The Mystery of the Downs

Mary Roberts Rinehart
Sight Unseen and The Confession

Dorothy L. Sayers
Whose Body?

Sir William Magnay
The Hunt Ball Mystery

Mabel and Paul Thorne
The Sheridan Road Mystery

Louis Tracy
The Strange Case of Mortimer Fenley
The Albert Gate Mystery
The Bartlett Mystery
The Postmaster's Daughter
The House of Peril
The Sandling Case: What Would You Have Done?
Charles Edmonds Walk
The Paternoster Ruby

John R. Watson
The Mystery of the Downs
The Hampstead Mystery

Edgar Wallace
The Daffodil Mystery
The Crimson Circle

Carolyn Wells
Vicky Van
The Man Who Fell Through the Earth
In the Onyx Lobby
Raspberry Jam
The Clue
The Room with the Tassels
The Vanishing of Betty Varian
The Mystery Girl
The White Alley
The Curved Blades
Anybody but Anne
The Bride of a Moment
Faulkner's Folly
The Diamond Pin
The Gold Bag
The Mystery of the Sycamore
The Come Backy